ROSE OF SKIBBEREEN

BOOK 4: ROSIE

By John McDonnell

Copyright © 2014 John McDonnell

ISBN-13: 9798649127363

Discover other titles at John McDonnell's Amazon page:
amazon.com/author/johnmcdonnell

FOREWORD

This is Book Four in the "Rose Of Skibbereen" series, a group of fictional stories about Rose Sullivan from Skibbereen, County Cork, Ireland. Here is a synopsis of the story so far:

Rose came to Philadelphia in 1880 to work as a domestic servant so she could send money back to her impoverished family in Skibbereen. She planned to stay in Philadelphia for ten years, but that plan changed when she married a man named Peter Morley.

Peter Morley was not his real name, however. His name was Sean McCarthy, but when he killed a British Army officer in Ireland he ran away to America and changed his name. He became a coachman for a wealthy family in Philadelphia, and that is where he met and married Rose.

It was a troubled marriage. Peter Morley was a restless man, always looking to recreate himself in this fast-changing country of America. He felt trapped in his marriage to Rose, and after fathering three children with her, he abandoned her on New Year's Day of 1900. He had fallen in love with a woman named Edith Jones, and he told her his name was James Francis. He never told her about his wife Rose. He married Edith, moved to a different part of Philadelphia, and had two children with her. Although he lived not far from Rose in the city, their paths never crossed again in life.

Peter (or James) died in 1935 and Rose in 1960. Edith died in 1961.

Here are the characters that have been affected by the lives of Rose and Peter:

Paul Morley. Born in 1891, he is the son of Rose and Peter. His two brothers, Willy and Tim, died young. He married Lucy Campbell and had two children with her. He was a successful businessman, but he got in trouble during World War II through his ties to a Nazi sympathizer. He cheated on Lucy, lost his business, and spent five years in prison for tax evasion.

Lucy Morley. Born in 1893, she is Paul's wife. Her world was shattered when Paul went astray in the 1940s, and especially when she found out he had been cheating on her, and she has taken a long time to recover from it. She still has a deep-seated mistrust of Paul, although she deals with it by throwing herself into the Civil Rights movement.

Rosie Morley. Born in 1927, she is the daughter of Paul and Lucy Morley. She is a singer and a dreamer, and improvises her way through life. She has passion and enthusiasm, but makes many mistakes because of her rash nature.

Billy Morley. Born in 1930, the son of Paul and Lucy, he enlisted in the U.S. Navy just after World War II and has spent many years as a career Navy man, far away from Philadelphia. He was traumatized by his childhood, when his father Paul had his public disgrace, and he stays away from the family.

Pete Morley. Born in 1946, he is the son of Rosie Morley and a British naval officer named James Charlesworth. Rosie does not know that Charlesworth is the grandson of the British officer her grandfather Peter killed back in Ireland in the late 1800s. Her romance with Charlesworth only lasted till the end of 1945. That is when James Charlesworth went back to England after the war, leaving Rosie to raise the infant Pete on her own.

James Charlesworth. Rosie's lover during World War II. When this part of the story starts he is living in London with his wife, but his marriage is a loveless one.

Edith Francis (Jones). Born in 1876. She came from England to Philadelphia in 1900, where she met a handsome Irishman who said his name was James Francis. She did not find out till he died in 1935 that he had another identity. He was Sean McCarthy, who had killed a man in Ireland and fled to America, where he changed his name to Peter Morley. In America he had married Rose Sullivan and fathered three sons with her, then abandoned his family. Edith Jones was bitter for years about his deception, but she later found happiness with a man named Simon Levin, and she moved with him to Israel in the late 1940s. She died in 1961.

Mercy Francis. Born in 1902. Her parents were Edith and James Francis (Peter Morley). She never recovered from finding out that her father had lied about his identity and so much else in his life. She left Philadelphia in the 1940s and moved around the country, marrying and divorcing several times, never settling anywhere for long.

John Francis. His parents were Edith and James. Born in 1904. He died in a shipyard accident during World War II.

This part of the story starts in 1961.

CHAPTER ONE

June 1961

Rosie knew it was the dream again. Maybe this time she could find out where the music was coming from. It was like nothing she had ever heard before, a sweetness and a note of sadness, a lilt, a yearning, harmonies that would shiver your heart with their beauty, and a beat that would slow to the pace of a dirge, then speed up with a wild intensity that made you feel like your heart was bursting.

It was more than sound -- she saw it as well as heard it. The music went through her; she felt it in her being, a feeling of being alive, like she had never really lived till she heard that music.

It was always the same. She was in a world of green, a place of distant mountains with curtains of mist hanging over them, the roar of the sea crashing on a rocky shore in the distance, great trees with their arms outstretched as if pleading for mercy, and always, that music.

It was coming from down in the glen, down there where the stream ran through the valley like a ribbon of silver, down there where the trees grew along the riverbank, where there seemed to be movement and dancing going on. She had to get down there and hear more of it, tap her feet to it, dance to it, perhaps even open her mouth and the notes, those magical notes, would come out clear as a bell and sweet as honey, as if she'd known them all along.

She would start down the mountain, toward the sound of the music, wondering who was making it, what instruments were they using, how could they sing notes so high and sweet and yet with a ragged edge too, a balancing on the edge of being flat, out of tune, somehow pulling together just in time to make a sound like nothing on this Earth?

She would start down the hillside, across the broken ground, tasting the salt air in her mouth, feeling the wind in her hair, and after a bit she would be running, running across the uneven ground, knowing that she had to get there fast before the music stopped, before the magic disappeared like morning dew when the sun came up.

And then, utter, deafening silence.

She felt like a baby being pulled away from its mother's breast. Suddenly it was all gone. She was standing on the side of the mountain but the trees were gone, the music was gone, everything was gone. It had all disappeared.

This had happened so many times before. This dream with the magical music had come to her so many times before but she had never been able to get down the side of the mountain in time to see who was playing those sounds.

The silence was raw and offensive to her, it was like something sordid. She ached with her whole body to hear that music again.

But there was nothing, a vacuum, a windswept vista with not a soul around.

Slowly she came back to consciousness, feeling the heat of the summer night, the sweat on her body as she lay in bed with only the fan blowing hot air on her.

Like always, it was painful to come back to the reality of who she was and where. She wanted to be in that green land with that music playing so much. She belonged there, but she realized now with sadness that it was just beyond her reach, fading away again.

Then, as she awoke, there was another sound that came to her, also sweet but a pale shadow of what she had heard in her dream. Even so, it filled her with happiness. Any music was better than that awful silence; any music could make her forget her loneliness.

It was the sound of voices blended together in harmony. The boys in the neighborhood were singing again, crooning their street corner harmony down in the courtyard where the brick and stone and metal of the houses would give their teenage voices the most resonance.

The alarm clock on her nightstand said ten minutes to midnight, and she knew she should go back to sleep, because she had to get up at 5:30 in the morning to get to her waitress job at the diner. It was hard enough getting up in the dark to go to that job but if she got out of bed and went down to the courtyard she wouldn't be back for an hour at least, and she'd be bleary eyed and exhausted serving all the working men their eggs and coffee in the morning.

But then she heard the lead singer's voice soaring, like a bell tone cutting through the other voices; the clear high tenor that she knew was Bobby Juliano.

That boy was going to go places, she knew it. His voice was special, different than the others. It had a worldly ache to it that was unusual in one so young. He was just a boy, barely 20 years old, but his voice had the weary grace of someone twice his age.

He lived down the street with his mother, and although they were poor he was a happy-go-lucky kid, always smiling and joking. He had dusky skin and curly brown hair, with eyes as green as emeralds. He never knew his father, and the rumor in the neighborhood was that his father was a black man. Bobby worked in the Italian Market selling fish and he knew every customer by name. He smiled readily and remembered everybody's name. And when he opened his mouth to sing! It was like the angels had sent one of their own to let us earthbound souls hear what Heaven sounds like.

Rosie couldn't stay in bed, not when sounds like that were coming through her open window.

She threw the sheet off and pulled on a pair of jeans underneath her nightgown, and ran next door to the bedroom where her son Pete slept. "Come on, sleepyhead, the boys are singing downstairs. Let's go hear them!"

Pete opened one eye and mumbled, "Aw, Mom, stop. I have school tomorrow, you know that. I can't be up till all hours singing doo wop."

"Come on, don't be a stick in the mud," Rosie said, pulling on his arm. "How many times do you get to hear sounds like that? Those guys are going to be famous someday, and you can say you heard them first."

Rosie pulled the covers off Pete's foot and tickled it.

"Mom, stop!" he shouted, giggling and pulling his foot away. "I have a math test tomorrow. I need my sleep."

But it was too late. She always knew tickling his feet could get him to stop being so grim. He was the most serious boy she ever knew, and she wished he could be more carefree, the way she was.

He sat up, still sleepy. "Okay," he said, rubbing his eyes. "I'll come downstairs for fifteen minutes. Then I have to go back to sleep. Those guys down there don't care about school. Half of them dropped out anyway. I don't want to work in the market like Bobby Juliano, so I need my high school degree."

"Oh, stop being such a drip," Rosie said. "You only live once. You have to appreciate harmony like that, Pete. Come on, put some clothes on and let's go downstairs."

Pete pulled on some pants and slippers and got out of bed and they raced down the steps of the apartment building and out to the narrow back alley that opened on a courtyard.

When they got there, the boys were singing in the center of the courtyard, bathed in a halo of moonlight with a group of other kids standing around. It was magical. They were singing "Why Do Fools Fall In Love," the Frankie Lymon and the Teenagers song from a few years before. There were three background singers and Bobby Juliano, and he had a voice that soared and swooped like Lymon's but it had more ache in it, more loss and loneliness, and it sent shivers down Rosie's spine.

Why do fools fall in love?

Why do birds sing so gay?

And lovers await the break of day

Why do they fall in love?

It was the eternal lament of the lover who can't figure out what's happening to him, why he is once again acting the fool, pulled forward by his heart against the current of his wisdom.

And then:

Why does my heart skip this crazy beat?

For I know, it will reach defeat

Tell me why, tell me why?

Why do fools fall in love?

It was the question we all ask deep in our hearts in the middle of the night, and Bobby's voice contained the urgency, puzzlement, and resignation that Rosie felt. On that last "Why?" Bobby's voice had a catch in it like he was stifling a sob, and it made Rosie's eyes sting with bitterness. Why indeed? Why did she keep falling in love, as if she'd never learned the simple lesson that it always ended badly, it always ended in defeat. There was no other way, it seemed.

This boy, how was he able to sing of these things when he was barely more than a boy? Although he had rock hard arms from lifting crates of fish packed in ice all day, he still had a wisp of fuzz on his cheeks, and a shy smile like a teenager. And yet, his voice had so much wisdom and hurt in it, as if he were a very old soul.

Rosie looked around and saw the girls were all looking at Bobby Juliano. She knew the power a singer can have on an audience: she'd felt it many times when she used to sing with jazz bands years ago. It didn't happen so much now, because the big bands had gone out of style and the kids wanted to listen to rock n' roll these days. Her singing now was limited to recording advertising jingles for the agencies in town, some wedding gigs with one of the few remaining orchestras in the city, and once in awhile she'd get a call to sing background at one of the recording studios in New York.

But she knew the times had changed, and this new music was where the energy was. It was so alive, so vital, with the pounding beat and the schoolboy harmonies, and it was so -- young! She felt young still, even though she was past 30, but she still wanted to be part of that. She didn't want the door to close on her youth; she was determined to keep it open no matter what happened.

The boys ended with a rousing, final, "Why do fools fall in love?" and the bass singer dipped down to subterranean levels while Bobby soared high above. There was an instant of silence, and then wild applause from the kids. Rosie whooped and hollered with the rest of them, clapping so hard that Pete nudged her in embarrassment.

"Sing another!" she said. "Come on, do 'Great Pretender' by the Platters."

Bobby smiled shyly and said, "Miss Morley, you know we need a girl singer for that one. Would you like to join us?"

"I thought you'd never ask," Rosie said, and took her place next to the three boys standing behind Bobby.

Bobby launched into the words to "Great Pretender", the Platters hit.

Oh-oh, yes I'm the great pretender

Pretending that I'm doing well

My need is such I pretend too much

I'm lonely but no one can tell

Oh-oh, yes I'm the great pretender

Adrift in a world of my own

I've played the game but to my real shame

You've left me to grieve all alone

Instantly Rosie found the spot where her voice fit in with the others, locked in the harmony, and she sang happily in the background while Bobby's voice crooned the lyrics about a lover who was wearing a mask of happiness while his heart was broken. It was all so sad and sweet, and yet there was still that youthful energy, that vitality that Rosie knew was gone from the jazz of her time. These young hearts around her could be broken many a time, she knew, but that was better than living a life of drab conformity like so many other people her age. There had to be more to life than what she saw around her in the world of 1961. People everywhere with the same haircuts, the same clothes, the same jobs, the same houses - - it was maddening, and sometimes she wanted to stop them on the street and shake them out of their sameness. "Wake up!" she wanted to shout. "Wake up and do something crazy. Take your shoes off and run barefoot through the street! Eat ice cream for breakfast! Quit your stupid job and drive across the country. Do something to break out of the straitjacket you're in!"

Bobby wasn't going to be like that, she knew. He had too much potential. Anybody who could sing like that was going to be a big star. You had only to hear that voice, it echoed in your soul, you simply could not ignore that gorgeous tenor. It baffled her why no one had realized Bobby's talent yet.

When the song was finished, Rosie knew she should go back upstairs. For one thing, Pete was motioning for her to leave, and she knew he was hoping she would not embarrass him further by singing another song.

The way she acted around Bobby was especially embarrassing to him.

"Can't you act your age?" he had said once before, when he noticed how she looked at Bobby. "He's ten years younger than you, Mom. Stop it!"

The a cappella session had to end anyway, because a man in one of the upstairs apartments raised his window and shouted, "Hey, it's after midnight! People are trying to sleep. Quit all that racket, willya!"

"Yeah, I gotta go to bed," Bobby said. "Gotta be up early tomorrow to haul all them fish around. God, I hate smelling like fish!"

"You keep singing like that, and you'll sing your way out of the fish market," Rosie said.

"Thanks, Miss Morley," Bobby said, "but I don't know. Me and the boys made a demo record, but we haven't had much luck getting anyone to listen to it."

"That's a crime," Rosie said. "Listen, I'm going to do something for you. You know Howie Morse, the DJ?"

"Sure," Bobby said. "Everybody knows him. The 'Dittybopper', is what he calls himself. I listen to his radio show from New Jersey. His record hops are getting popular. I've only been to one, because I have to get up so early for work and they're too far away, but I know lots of kids who go to them."

"He comes to my diner for breakfast a lot," Rosie said. "He's a real night owl. He puts on those hops, then comes over to Philly to hang out with his record business pals all night, then comes in to the diner at 6 AM for his ham and eggs. You give me that record you made, and I'll make sure he takes it home with him."

"Really? You'd do that for us?"

"You bet I would. Just get me that record, and I'll get it to Howie Morse."

She saw Pete giving her a jaundiced look, but she didn't care. She just wanted to help this kid with the sweet voice, that's all.

At least, that's what she told herself.

CHAPTER TWO

It had all happened so fast. She had cornered the Dittybopper the next morning at the diner, while he was sitting with his pals at his corner table. The sun rising in New Jersey was shooting soft orange spears of light through the blue metal skeleton of the Walt Whitman bridge, but the Dittybopper couldn't see that, because he wore big black sunglasses and he sat with his back to the window so he could keep up a running commentary with everyone in earshot.

"Hey all you bippers, boppers, and tommyknockers, the Dittybopper is in your room. He's groomed, perfumed, and carryin' the tunes. Where's all my Buddhists, beats, trick or treats, my hep cats and ballin' Jacks? I'm here to tell you a change is comin' and it won't be slow, it's like a stack of dominos, man when it blows, everything goes. I can't sit down, I get around, I'm known all over town, I got the dits I got the dahs, I'm the Morse Code of bop, you gotta come to my record hops, I'm the man with the dream, I'm all over the scene, I got the wax you know the facts, the sound of a generation feeling its time, its time, it's time!!!"

He spit out words like bullets from a machine gun and he could keep it up constantly. He was like a motor with no Off switch, a caffeinated, hyperbolic hipster in a sharkskin suit with his slicked back hair so shiny you could see your reflection in it and shoes polished to a mirror brightness. He was a natural entertainer, a "personality", as he called himself, "a comer". The story was that he'd started as a gofer at the 500 Club in Atlantic City, and learned about the entertainment business from the tuxedoed stars like Sinatra and Dean Martin who played there, then struck out on his own as a DJ at a tiny little radio station in the Pine Barrens of South Jersey. He played a steady diet of vocal groups: the Cadillacs, the Chantels, the Clovers, the Duprees, the Flamingos, the Shirelles, the Spaniels, the Quotations, and lots more. He was a pint-sized guy with an ego the size of New Jersey, and ambition to go with it, and he was bound for the big time. He started putting on record hops in rented halls, and he built a following of teenagers eager to dance to the music he was playing on his radio show. As he got more popular he came over the bridge to Philadelphia to put on his shows, and he moved to a bigger station, the 50,000-watt WHAM. He strutted around like a little Napoleon, and he had already helped several local groups get record contracts, through his growing network of music industry insiders.

He had the look of someone who could rival Dick Clark, the smooth coiffed, mellifluous host of American Bandstand, the crosstown kingmaker who had a national audience for his afternoon TV show that played the latest hits for a studio audience of fresh-faced teenagers.

But the Dittybopper's entourage was not so clean cut. The guys who surrounded him were young Turks also, comers who were going places too, but some of them were going to the wrong places. They wore the same shiny suits and had the same slicked back haircuts, but they had cold eyes, a glint of malice to go with the play of light that flashed from their cufflinks and expensive watches. One of them, a man named Gaeton Russo, was a silent partner in the diner, and Rosie couldn't stand him. He was connected with the mob, and the diner was a hangout for his friends, a place where bulky men in immaculately pressed suits came to drink coffee and talk over their business deals in low voices.

Everybody knew Russo was bad news. He had already served time in prison and was rumored to be the muscle behind some payola that was going on, where radio DJs were being paid money to play certain records. A couple of local DJs had gotten their noses broken when they didn't play the right songs, and Russo was supposedly behind it. He skimmed money from every business he was in, including the diner, and Rosie detested him.

He had roving hands and was touchy with the waitresses, and the girls who protested were fired within a day. There was something creepy about him: he had bullet gray eyes and wore pancake makeup to cover his five o'clock shadow, and he thought of himself as a ladies' man. Russo had an Achilles heel, though. He had a wife, a slim blonde named Gina, and he was a different man around her -- his cool facade cracked, and he looked nervous and vulnerable. Gina liked to flirt, which enraged him, and he kept his eyes fixed on her at all times, to make sure she wasn't making eyes at some strange man.

So that morning after Rosie made sure that Russo was in the Men's Room, and after she gave the Dittybopper his ham and eggs, coffee black with just a splash of skim in it, hash browns and toast, and he interrupted his patter long enough to flirt with her for a moment or two, she slipped the envelope with the black 45 RPM homemade record in it next to his plate.

"What's this, darling?" he said, raising an eyebrow.

"It's the next big singer to come from Philly," she said. "He's got a voice that's better than anything you've ever heard, and this is a demo record he made. Listen to it when you get a chance; you won't regret it."

He pushed the envelope back over the table. "Another kid who wants to be a star, huh? What are you, his mother? I'm sorry, honey, I'm a busy man. Do you know how many people I got pushin' vinyl at me? I used to listen to 'em all, but they're all crapola, just rank garbage, a waste of my time. I'm sorry, lady, but tell your son to go call Dick Clark. He's always looking for another Fabian."

"I'm not his mother!" Rosie snapped. She reached over and pulled off the Dittybopper's sunglasses, leaving him blinking like a mole that's been pulled out of its tunnel. "There, maybe now you can see that I'm not old enough to be the mother of a 20-year-old."

"Hey, give me back my shades," the Dittybopper said, reaching for them.

Rosie knew she didn't have much time before Russo came back, and already some of the seedier members of the entourage had interrupted their conversations to stare at her, so she talked fast.

"Listen, Howie, you won't regret this. This kid can sing rings around every crooner you've heard. He's only 20 and he's shy, so nobody knows him outside the neighborhood. You could break a big star right here in Philly -- think of what that could do for your career! He's the real thing, I guarantee you."

"What's going on here?"

That voice sent a chill down Rosie's spine, and she turned to see Russo eyeing her with suspicion.

"Is this broad bothering you, Howie?" Russo said.

There was an agonizingly long silence, when Rosie saw the malice up close in Russo's eyes.

Finally, Morse reached over and took his glasses back from Rosie, then put them on and smiled. "No, my man, she's no problem," he said. "No problem at all. Just a lady who's trying to do a favor for a neighborhood kid. Says he's got a good voice and I should hear it. Who knows, maybe he really can sing enough to make the girls swoon, huh? Man, that's what we're all looking for, right? Those boy singers that make the girls get all dreamy eyed and soft in the knees, the ones with those voices that make the girls cry, the mothers sigh, and the fathers say, 'Why?'." He laughed his rat-a-tat machine gun laugh. "Sure, I'll take a listen, and if I like, I'll come back tomorrow and ask you how to find this Mr. Wonderful. Okay? Is that good?"

"It's fine," Rosie said, breathing again. "Just fine." She made a beeline for the kitchen, feeling Russo's eyes on the back of her head as she went.

Rosie had taken a big chance that day, but for awhile she felt like it had paid off. The next morning at 6:00 the Dittybopper strutted in with his people, and he couldn't wait to talk to her.

"There she is, the girl with the golden ears! Fellows, this woman has ears like a solid gold artist. She should work for Capital or RCA Records, make a million bucks for them signing talent off the streets. She's got the moxie to find a diamond in the rough, a boy nobody heard of who can sing like an angel. Sit down, darling, I need to talk to you."

Rosie sat down across from the Dittybopper, with Russo next to him fixing her with his steely gaze, and she listened as the Dittybopper told her that this Juliano kid had a voice with star quality, a "one in a million set of pipes, a voice that's going to make the girls turn themselves inside out trying to get to him, like bees to honey, baby, like bees to honey." He laid it all out: how the kid would be featured at his next record hop, how he'd get a record deal for him and the vocal group, how by this time next year he could be a national star, "maybe sooner, if we're lucky and find some good songwriters to produce material for him."

"What's he look like?" the Dittybopper said. "'Cause that's as important as his voice. Is he a heartthrob, a cruiser, a boy who'll bruise the hearts of every girl in town?"

"He's a good-looking kid," Rosie said. "No, better than that: he's got soft green eyes and brown curly hair and a killer shy smile. He makes your heart skip a beat," she continued, thinking of how her own heart got a lift just being around him.

The Dittybopper leaned over close to her. "Is he white?"

"His mother is," Rosie said, taken aback. "His Dad isn't around. I think he was a Negro, but I'm not sure."

The Dittybopper paused for just a second, then said, "Can he pass for white?"

"Why? There are lots of Negro groups with hit records. That shouldn't be a problem."

"Shouldn't be but sometimes is," the Dittybopper said. "Especially in the South. Can he pass?"

"He looks Italian, and he uses his mother's last name, Juliano," Rosie said. "And the other guys in the group are Italian."

"Perfect!" the Dittybopper said. "I want to meet this cat."

CHAPTER THREE

October 1962

"My dear, I have a job for you, but it involves going to Philadelphia" Nelson Parnell said.

"No," Mercy said. "I told you before, I'll go anywhere but there. That's off limits."

Parnell was standing on the balcony of his hacienda style house in La Jolla, looking over the vast blue Pacific as he sipped a glass of white wine. He looked like a film star, with his silver hair swept back off his forehead, his deeply tanned face and his still trim body in a black V-neck sweater and a pair of white slacks.

Mercy Francis was sitting on his plush white couch in his living room, facing him, drinking her own glass of white wine. She was ten years younger than him at 58, although Nelson looked about the same age as her. He had been a film actor in his youth, during the Silent Era, and he had learned at an early age to pay close attention to his appearance, which paid dividends, as he liked to say, now that he was an art dealer for the rich and powerful in Hollywood.

"My clients don't want to deal with an old man," he'd often say. "California is the land of illusion, and we must keep up appearances."

Mercy was his assistant, bookkeeper, researcher, and all-around Girl Friday, although she certainly wasn't a girl anymore. She had answered an ad to work in his art gallery ten years ago, after her third marriage broke up, and she had quickly proven herself indispensable to him.

It was easy, really. Like Parnell, she had no family, and could work long hours. He had never married, for the simple reason that he was gay, a fact that had hurt his film career when he was involved in a scandal in the 1920s, but had helped him in other ways. He had been plugged in to a network of other gay men in the film capital for decades, and when he started a new career as an art dealer in the 1930s they proved to be a ready market for him.

Mercy was not gay, but she was like a shipwrecked sailor who had somehow found herself washed up on a palm tree lined beach when she thought she was a goner. She was so happy for one more chance at Life that she was willing to do anything in gratitude to the man who had saved her.

She had worked herself up to the point where she traveled the country for Parnell, meeting with representatives of his various clients, evaluating new artists, buying works, and lately, in response to his growing collectibles business, she had visited estates and even bid on items in auctions for him and his clients.

But not Philadelphia. She would not go there. "I grew up there and I have bad memories," is all she would say when Parnell asked. "I just don't like the place, that's all, and I won't go back."

Until now he had respected her wishes, traveling to Philadelphia himself when business required it, but never asking her to go.

This time, though, he could not go.

"Mercy," he said, coming over to her and sitting next to her on the couch. "You know we have a big show in two weeks for that sculptor Andy Branch, the one I've been grooming for awhile. It is impossible for me to leave, not this close to the show. This could be the biggest thing in the LA art market in a decade. I can't leave. I need you to do this."

"Can't it wait?" she said.

"No," he said, putting down his wine glass on the carved redwood coffee table. "This is for a big client, and he insists that there's something in Philadelphia he's interested in. He would go himself, but he's a big movie star out here, and he doesn't want to attract attention. He's mad to get his hands on this stuff, and he wants us to go sniff it out for him. Apparently he's afraid some other collector will get there first. Time is of the essence."

"What is it?" Mercy said. "What is this stuff he's so interested in?"

"Old films," Parnell said. "Really old stuff, two reelers from before the First World War, if you can believe they actually made films back then. From the dawn of film, apparently."

Mercy was suspicious. "Who made these films?"

"A gentleman named Lubin. Siegmund Lubin."

Mercy felt sick. "Lubin? No." She stood up. "I'm not going, Nelson. You can fire me if you want, but I'm not going to take that assignment."

She was trembling, her knees were shaking, and Parnell stood up and came to her, putting his arm around her. "What is the matter?" he said. "You're shaking like a leaf, Mercy. I've never seen you like this. Do you have some connection to this man?"

She exhaled. "No. I mean, yes. I guess you could say I do have a connection to Lubin. Long ago, when I was a girl."

"Then this should be a special thing for you," Parnell said. "Reconnecting with your past, and all that. Actually, I've never heard you talk about your childhood, Mercy."

"There's a reason," she snapped. "It wasn't a very pleasant one. My memories are not good ones, Nelson. And I have no interest in reconnecting with them." She turned to leave. "I'm not going back there.

Parnell grabbed her arm. "Please, Mercy. Sit down, please. I need to tell you something."

Mercy sat down reluctantly, and Nelson sat across from her on the coffee table, so he could look into her eyes.

"I'm sorry this is a painful subject for you," he said. "But I need you desperately right now. This, ah, client, is a close friend of mine. Very close. Our relationship is a secret, though, because it would ruin his career if it were known that he, ah, consorted with people like me. He's developed this obsession with early cinema history, and he has been collecting old movies, posters, equipment and the like for many years. He wants to buy some of Lubin's films because it will complete his collection. I want to help him, because, well, what do you do for people you love? You try to make them happy."

"Just get somebody else to go back East," Mercy said. "I'm sure you can find someone else to do this."

"Of course I could," Parnell said. "But they wouldn't be as good as you."

"Flattery will get you nowhere. I'm not going." She stood up again. "There's nothing you can say that will change my mind, Nelson. Now, excuse me, but I have to go."

He grabbed her wrist again. "Please, sit down. I need to tell you something."

She sat down, ready to refuse him again.

He shrugged his shoulders. "Okay, I guess I'm going to have to tell you the truth. There is no movie star client, Mercy. This is for me." He took her hand in his. "I never told you this before, but when I hired you ten years ago, I was at a desperate place in my life. Not since that little scandal back in the 1920s did I feel so hopeless. I had just broken up with a man who'd paid back my love and generosity by stealing everything that wasn't nailed down in my house and some of the most expensive pieces in my gallery. I wasn't carrying enough insurance to cushion the fall, and it almost bankrupted me. I lost clients over it, I lost the house I had been living in since the 1930s, and more importantly, I lost my will to live. I just didn't see the point of going on, when all you could expect was more heartache and wounds. It wasn't the first time this had happened to me -- although nobody had ever done such a thorough job of cleaning me out -- and I figured it wouldn't be the last. I was ready to just pack it all in, jump off the edge of a cliff and do a gorgeous swan dive into the Pacific.

"Then one night it occurred to me that if I ended it all I'd be leaving a mountain of debts, and I don't like not paying my debts -- I take pride in that, you know. I didn't want to be remembered as a deadbeat. So, I dragged myself back up on my feet and decided to keep plugging away till I somehow got everybody paid off, and then I would kill myself.

"There was no joy in the business for me anymore -- I was only working to build things up again so that I could pay my creditors. I had no idea how I would do it, and half the time I still got the urge to throw in the towel and just quit.

"And then something happened. I met this wonderful woman who applied for a job with me, and who became a good friend totally unexpectedly. She came to me at a low point in my life and lifted me up, and she gave me a reason for living again. That was you, Mercy. You're named appropriately, because you brought mercy to my life." His eyes were glistening with tears and he smiled. "I value every day with you, and I thank you for bringing me back to the land of the living." He squeezed her hand.

"Stop it, Nelson," she said, "or you're going to get me crying, and you know I don't like to cry. I appreciate what you said, and you know I love you, but what does this have to do with me going to Philadelphia?"

He sighed. "Okay, time for more truth. I have an, ah, incurable condition." He paused to take a cigarette out of a pack of Camels on the coffee table, and he lit it with a gold embossed lighter he took out of his pocket.

"What?" she said. "What are you talking about?"

He paused for a moment, looking at the sunset over the ocean. Then, he exhaled a stream of smoke, looked at the cigarette, and said: "You know, I started smoking these damned things as a teenager, and by the time I was in my 40s doctors were saying they thought smoking caused lung cancer. I tried dozens of times to give them up, but I couldn't."

He looked Mercy in the eye. "I've been to see the folks at Cedars of Lebanon hospital recently, Mercy, and they tell me that I have lung cancer. There's not much they can do in these cases, so my time is limited."

Mercy gasped. "No, Nelson, don't say that. There must be something they can do!"

He shrugged his shoulders and took another drag on his cigarette, then blew out the smoke. "Oh, they've offered some solutions," he said, after a moment. "But they sound pretty ghastly to me. I don't want them cutting me up like a piece of steak just so I can survive a few more months. It's the same thing with the radiation therapy or the drug treatments they told me about. I'm not interested in spending my days throwing up my breakfast, lunch and dinner, just to eke out a few miserable months more of existence." He swept his glance around the room, taking in the sculpture, the blue and white Chinese vases, the Oriental rugs, the modern art on every wall, the tasteful furniture. "I've had a good run, Mercy, and I can't complain. My life is filled with beauty, and I am a happy man. I have no wish to be greedy. No, I'll keep working at the gallery as long as I'm able to, and then I'll fade out, just like an old two reeler.

"But this is where you come in. For several years now I've been collecting prints of silent films, mostly out of nostalgia for my youth. Well, as you might think, since I got this diagnosis my interest has gotten more intense. It's become important to me to find every film that I appeared in, even if I only had a bit part in it. I never told you this, but I grew up in Baltimore, and when I was a young man I spent some time in Philadelphia. I got a job as a laborer at Lubin's original studio at 20th and Indiana streets. The old man took a liking to me, and he started finding me roles in his short films. I was good at it, and that's how my acting career started.

"So you see," he added, "I have a connection to Lubin too."

He stubbed out his cigarette in a porcelain ashtray, and continued: "I didn't stick around long, though. I was footloose and fancy-free back then, and I moved around a lot, usually following some attractive young man. Anyway, I ended up in California before the First World War, and I found my way to one of the studios out here, told them I had experience in motion pictures back East, and the rest is history."

"That's quite a story," Mercy said. "So what you're saying is: this is all for you, for your legacy?"

"Yes," he said. "I have bought or bartered my way to a collection of prints that document my silent film career, and I have almost all of what's available, stored in a vault in downtown Los Angeles. There are some holes in my collection, but the biggest ones are the smattering of films I made for Lubin. I don't have any of them, and I'd like to get my hands on some. There's a bit of urgency, though. You know the Museum of Modern Art in New York has an archive of old silent films, and I've heard through the grapevine they're sniffing around Southeastern Pennsylvania looking for the Lubin films. That's why I need you to go now."

Mercy sighed. "I wish you wouldn't ask me to do this. Anything but this."

"But why?" he said. "We all have unpleasant memories from our past. I don't understand why--"

"Because my father worked for Lubin," she snapped. "I hate even saying that man's name."

Nelson started at her words. "He worked for Pops Lubin? When? What did he do?"

"He was Lubin's driver for a few years," she said. "Probably around the same time you were there. Then he worked his way into bit parts in some of the films. I think he thought he was going to be a star, and it went to his head. He got pretty full of himself."

Even after all these years it hurt to talk about her father, and she turned away with her eyes burning.

"I'm sorry," Nelson said, stroking her hand. "What was his name? Maybe I knew him. Hell, maybe I played a scene or two with him."

"We knew him as James Francis. We found out later he had been married before, and he had other names."

Nelson squinted, trying to remember. "I think I remember Lubin's driver. A big Irishman who laughed a lot. Good singing voice, right?"

"That was him," Mercy said. "The life of the party. Did you know him?"

"I don't remember much about him," Nelson said, shaking his head. "I was just a kid. I don't think he was in any of my films. It was a long time ago, Mercy. I'm sorry. So this is why you don't want to go back to Philadelphia?"

Mercy sighed and looked out at the blue Pacific, stretching for miles to the horizon. The sky was a deep purple above, shading to a light blue mixed with a few orange rays from the setting sun near the horizon. She could see the lights of commercial ships far out at sea. It seemed her whole adult life had been pointing West, and she liked that direction. She had left Philadelphia at the beginning of the War and moved around quite a bit in the 20 years since then, but always her next move had been west. She had never wanted to go back east, not ever. Her mother Edith sent letters asking her to come back, but she'd always had a reason not to. Her brother John had died during the war, and even though she sometimes felt guilty for abandoning her mother, she could not go back to that city.

It had nothing to do with her mother: Edith didn't even live there anymore, she had moved to Israel in 1959 with her second husband. Now she was gone too -- just last year Mercy had gotten a telegram from Israel telling her that Edith had died suddenly. Mercy wired back that she could not go to the funeral. The past was a painful place for her, and she did not want to see anyone connected with it.

Even though she had no connection to Philadelphia anymore, she still couldn't go back. What did she expect to see there? The ghost of her father? Well, not a ghost, but perhaps something worse than that -- a memory. Ghosts don't come out in the daylight, but memories are there all the time. A memory that was etched in her mind, of her father kissing a strange woman on the set of one of Lubin's movies, when she was a little girl. Her father, the man who had brought so much life, so much joy, into her world, the tall, handsome man with the radiant smile who had called her his little sweet potato, he had betrayed her. In one moment her childhood was

29

taken away from her, and she had never truly loved or believed in anything again.

"I have bad memories," she said, finally. "That's all. I've been running from them for years, I guess. I left home during the War, and I've been moving farther away ever since. I never wanted to go back."

Nelson put his hands on his knees and stood up. "Okay, now I understand. We all have places we don't want to go. I'll get someone else to do it."

"No!" Mercy said, surprising herself with how loud she said it. "No, I'll do it. I can face this for you, Nelson. You've been a bright light in my life, and I won't let you down. I'll go out there."

"But Mercy," Nelson said. "Don't forget, you're probably going to have to look at these films, if you find any. I'm specifically interested in ones that I made, but what if you find one with your father in it?"

She grimaced. "I don't know. I'll deal with it if it happens. Don't worry, I can handle this. If you want these films, I'll find them."

CHAPTER FOUR

1962

It went fast from that point, like a bullet out of a gun. Within a week the Dittybopper had Bobby and his group, renamed the Heartthrobs, singing at a record hop in New Jersey, where they went over big with the girls. Rosie was there -- Bobby asked her to come along -- and she saw the look in the girls' eyes. She knew the Dittybopper was seeing it too.

And so was Russo, who was standing in the wings with his boys. And Gina.

Gina didn't like staying home at night, and when she heard that Russo was going to a record hop with his friends to check out a new talent, she insisted on going. She was standing there in a fur stole and a spangled low cut black dress, dripping with jewelry, and she looked as out of place as a tuxedo on top of a poodle skirt. The kids were clean cut but Russo and Gina were the opposite, with eyes that were dead to the innocence of youth.

But her eyes were on Bobby. It was obvious she liked what she saw, the way she ran her eyes all over his body. Russo saw her staring, and his mouth became a hard, tight line that only got tighter when she went over to Bobby after the performance, elbowing some of the teenage girls out of the way, and spoke to him in her low, purring voice. Russo took as much as he could of this, then walked over and grabbed her arm and pulled her away, looking like he wanted to slug her right there.

The next six months were a whirlwind of hops, auditions, publicity appearances -- anything the Dittybopper could think of to get some traction for his budding star. He was more hyperkinetic than ever, talking faster and louder and seeming to need less and less sleep. At each appearance it was obvious Bobby was making more of an impact with the audience, especially the girls, and the momentum was starting to build. From New Jersey they had progressed to Philly, and then they started driving up to New York for bigger hops, opening for bigger name groups and sometimes stealing the show from them.

The girls were crazy for Bobby, and it was getting to the point where they were almost attacking him after the shows. He laughed and still acted shy, but Rosie could tell he enjoyed it. He was just a poor kid who never had much in his life, and now all of a sudden he was getting success by the handful, and he was riding the wave. Rosie often found him in a corner kissing some teenage fan, and she realized with some wistfulness that what she had done for him with the Dittybopper meant she would never have him to herself again. She contented herself with being a sort of stage mother for him, making sure he got to his appointments on time, pressing his suits, trying to make sure he ate healthy and got enough sleep.

She tried not to think of how young and beautiful he was.

Gina seemed more attracted to him every day, and Russo was going out of his mind with jealousy. The look of pure hatred in his eyes when Bobby was on stage was frightening. He was always trying to make fun of the kid, calling him "Lover Boy" and "Fruitcake", but nothing got Bobby rattled. He was grateful for what was happening to him, and he was just too happy to let a creep like Gaeton Russo bother him.

Russo didn't give up, though, even telling the Dittybopper he thought the kid was going nowhere, and Morse was wasting time with him. "He's a flash in the pan," he said. "He'll be lucky to have one hit, and then he'll be gone. You mark my words, Howie. He'll be back in the fish market by this time next year. And you're gonna look like a chump for spending so much time on this loser."

"And there you are wrong, my man," the Dittybopper would say. "This boy has star quality. He's got the stuff, the magic, the indefinable something that makes the girls go gaga and the parents scratch their heads in wonder. I'm telling you, it's not something the older generation can understand, but the Dittybopper has the antennae to receive this signal, this rockin' sound that will forever change the landscape of the teenage world."

It had to happen, Rosie thought, looking back on it. Bobby and Russo were on a collision course, and there was nothing anybody could do to stop it.

But it still was a shock when it happened.

Russo had to go out of town for a week on "business", and he gave strict instructions to Gina not to go to any of Bobby's concerts. She told him yes, but within a day she was squiring the boy all around town in her baby blue Cadillac, taking him to the best restaurants and supper clubs. She took him dancing, she took him shopping to buy a new suit, she stood in the wings and watched him sing with eyes that were more cynical than the adoring teenage girls but no less fascinated with him.

Rosie tried to tell him to watch out for her, but he didn't listen. He was young, full of beans, and he didn't think anything could hurt him.

But Russo had too many people watching Gina, and when he came back, it didn't take long for him to find out what had happened.

Rosie was upstairs in her kitchen frying hamburgers for dinner when Pete came bursting through the door.

"Mom, come quick, Bobby Juliano's hurt!"

She dropped the metal spatula on the linoleum floor and ran downstairs to the Juliano's apartment, where she could hear screaming inside.

She opened the door and saw blood everywhere. Bobby's mother was wailing almost incoherently, and she was crouched over Bobby's prone body.

"My God, is he dead?" Rosie said. "What happened?"

"Why, why did they do this to my son?" his mother screamed. "Why?"

"What happened?" Rosie repeated. She could see Bobby holding a blood-soaked towel to his face, so she knew he wasn't dead, at least. But there was blood everywhere, on the floor, the furniture, the walls. She knew he had to get to a hospital fast.

"Two men barged in here and attacked him," Bobby's mother said. "My son, who never did anything bad to anybody. They had knives. They cut his face. Why?"

"Help me get him up," Rosie said. "He needs to get to the hospital."

They bundled him into her car and she raced the ten blocks to the hospital, hustling straight past the front desk and into the Emergency Room. Bobby held her hand the whole time, but never said a word.

"Was it Russo?" she said.

He wouldn't answer, but she knew it was.

For the first time in her life she wanted to kill someone. She sat in the waiting room while the doctors worked on Bobby, and she thought of the ways she would kill Russo. She could buy a gun. She could stab him with a meat cleaver in the diner. She could poison him. She could hit him over the head with a baseball bat, and beat his evil body to a bloody pulp. Her hands shook with the desire to strangle him, to choke the life slowly out of him till his face turned purple and his eyes bulged out of his head.

I'll get him for this, she vowed. He won't get away with it.

The desire for revenge only got stronger when she finally got a good look at what Russo had done to Bobby. The doctors stitched the boy up, but he had an angry four inch scar running from his cheekbone to just below the left side of his mouth. It was a nasty looking thing, and it was going to kill his career. The popular music stars were all clean cut, smooth-faced boys and girls who looked like they just stepped off the dance floor at a record hop, and nobody, not even the edgier singers like Jerry Lee Lewis and Little Richard, looked like he had been on the losing end of a knife fight. Besides, it would take months for the wound to heal properly, and Bobby didn't have that kind of time. He needed to grab the brass ring now, when the time was right. You couldn't jump off the merry-go-round now and expect to get back on later. It would be too late, there would be some other handsome boy singer that had taken his place by then.

He knew it, too. "It's over," he said, when Rosie saw him in his hospital room. His face was bandaged up, but he was trying to make a joke of it all, trying to hide the hurt and disappointment inside.

"I'll just go back to the market," he said. "I was kind of missing those swordfish anyway. I'll sing my songs to the fish from now on. They're a better audience any day. I can't kiss them after the show, but at least they don't get jealous."

Gina never came to see him in the hospital. The Dittybopper came and tried to make light of it, telling Bobby that he'd be back on top "headlining the hops and pulling out all the stops," in no time, but everybody knew he was just putting on a show.

It was a crime, what happened, but Rosie knew she wouldn't get any justice unless she took matters into her own hands.

So she waited. It was hard to see Russo at the diner every day, to be so close to him, and not lash out. Her fingers itched to clasp him around his neck and squeeze, or to take a heavy plate and smash it across his skull.

But with reflection came a plan. This one was better, because it would hurt him more. She would turn him in to the police for something else, not what he did to Bobby. She knew he had his fingers dirty from so many shady deals, and she could get him sent away to prison, hopefully for a long time. The best part is she knew that Gina would be cheating on him the whole time he was away, and it would drive him crazy with jealousy.

Nobody from South Philadelphia would cross him, although many people had reason to want revenge on him. Rosie knew somebody, though, who might help her.

It was Millie, the bookkeeper at the diner, who hated Russo almost as much as Rosie did because he'd extorted money from her husband Abe years before when he owned a barber shop. Russo had been a young punk back then, and he roughed up Abe a few times when he'd been reluctant to pay his protection money. Millie swore that one of those beatings caused the heart problems that eventually killed Abe. Millie had already been doing the books at the diner when Russo bought his way in as a partner, and he never seemed to connect the dots, that she was Abe's widow.

"Too bad for him," Millie told Rose one day. "I've been watching him for awhile now, keeping track of all his dirty laundry. He thinks nobody knows what's going on, but I do."

Mille was the one who'd help, Rosie knew. She went to Millie after Bobby's slashing, and it didn't take much convincing to get Millie on her side. In fact, Millie offered a bonus: "I've been keeping a separate set of books for years, and I have it all recorded. I have the goods on him. I have it locked away in a safe in my house. He's done for."

They went to the IRS, to a gray building on Market street, and met with an agent named Ed Harrington, a tight-lipped man with a blonde crewcut who wore a short-sleeved white shirt and blue bow tie. They laid it all out, and they could tell from the look on his face that it was enough to get Russo for tax fraud.

"President Kennedy's brother Bobby's been trying to clean up this Mafia business," he said. "The evidence you brought in will help to take this gentleman out of circulation, and the government thanks you for that. You'll have to testify, of course," he said, looking closely at them. "Are you prepared to do that? Mr. Russo has a lot of associates that may not like what you're doing."

Rosie looked at Millie, who nodded her head. "I'm an old lady," she said. "How many years have I got left? Scum like Gaeton Russo don't scare me. I just want to see justice done."

"And you?" Harrington said, looking at Rosie.

"I'm not afraid," Rosie said, thinking of Bobby's slashed cheek. "He's gotten away with too much already. He needs to be stopped."

Rosie swallowed hard, though, hoping she could be as brave as Millie when the time came.

When the IRS agents arrested Russo, and the word got out that somebody had ratted on him, the Dittybopper came looking for Rosie.

He took her out in the alley behind the diner.

He snapped off his sunglasses and looked at her. "Did you turn him in?" he said, his voice like the splatter of hail on trash can lids. "I heard through the grapevine that it was somebody from the diner. Did you do it?"

"Why are you asking?" she said, sticking her chin out.

"Because I know you had a motive, little lady," he said. "I know you were in love with that boy singer, and I could see you wanting to get revenge for what my man Russo did to him. Did you do it?"

"What's the matter," Rosie said. "Are you scared they're gonna come after you too?"

The Dittybopper held his hands up. "I'm clean as a whistle, honey. The Dittybopper is a comer, and he knows better than to do anything that will affect his upward trajectory. No, I'm too smart for that, sweetie. Russo's a powerful cat, and I was happy to hang around with him, but I never got mixed up in any of his dirty business. He's just a good pal, that's all. A friend from the neighborhood, and you gotta stay loyal to your friends, right?

"But let me give you a word of advice," he continued, touching her on the shoulder. "If you turned him in, he'll find out. And he will come after you, and it won't be pretty what he does to you. He ruined Bobby's career, but at least the kid is still alive. That won't happen to you, young lady."

Rosie felt a sudden chill, and she shuddered.

"I would recommend very strongly that you get out of town, sweetheart," the Dittybopper continued. "Like now. And I would go far away, very far. In fact, I would go out of the country. Split the scene, you know? Let things cool down for awhile. Make yourself very scarce."

"I can't just pick up and leave," Rosie said. "I have a kid."

"Even more reason to go," he said. "And I would move the kid somewhere, if you can't take him with you. Make him disappear, you know what I mean? You must have cousins somewhere out in the sticks you can send him to. As for you, I'll tell you what I can do. I have a connection over in London, England. The music scene is happening over there, too, and I have a pal who works in the London office of Capitol Records. He can get you a job for a little while, get all the visa stuff straightened out. It's worth thinking about."

"London?" she said. "I've never been out of the country. I don't know. . ."

"It's a good idea," he said. "I recommend it highly. Think about it. You know where to find me, darling." He turned and walked away, leaving her shivering in the alley.

"Go!" She heard the voice as clear as if someone were standing behind her. She turned, but there was no one. The Dittybopper had disappeared into the back door of the diner, and the only sound was a passing car on the street.

Was it her imagination? No, as sure as she was standing there, a creature of solid bone, flesh and blood, she'd heard that voice. It had rung out like a bell. Was it God? A spirit? Her grandmother Rose had told her about her own mother's obsession with spirits and fairies back in Ireland. Did those things exist? Rosie had heard these voices before, but she'd always tried to ignore them, explain them away.

This time, she decided to listen.

CHAPTER FIVE

1962

It was after they buried her mother-in-law Rose Morley that Lucy found herself questioning what she'd done with her life. She admired the old woman, how she'd just stuck her head down and plowed forward, no matter what Life had thrown at her, and she'd survived it all, living to the age of 98.

She also realized, though, that the clock was ticking in her life, and what had she done?

She'd raised two frustrating children and been the wife of a man who cheated on her, a man who brought shame and embarrassment to the family by getting mixed up with Nazi sympathizers during World War II. Paul was 70 now, and although he had tried to make amends, the spark had gone out of their relationship. She looked at him and saw an old man with bristly white hair, blue eyes that were dimmed of the light that once shone in them, and hands that shook from the beginning stages of Parkinson's Disease. He tried to be cheerful and upbeat, wanted to be affectionate with her, but there was a wall between them now that would never go away.

Other women could take solace in their children, but even there Lucy was stymied. Her son Billy had joined the Navy as soon as he was old enough, just after the war ended, and he'd spent ten years sailing the world. He'd finally left the Navy a couple of years ago and put down stakes in Hawaii. She hadn't seen him since he came home after his discharge five years ago. He was no longer the moody teenager with a bad complexion who had gone away in 1947

-- now he was a 30 year old man with a military bearing, sure of himself but at the same time quite certain that he did not want to be a part of their lives anymore. He never came out and said that, but he made it clear that he was only back in Philadelphia for a short visit before he moved to Hawaii, and he would not be making these trips back East on a regular basis. He never invited Paul and Lucy to visit him in Hawaii, and he rarely answered her letters. He did not really exist for her now.

And Rosie! She was still around, but her life was a crazy, haphazard mess, scrambling from one job to another, one apartment to the next, one boyfriend after another. She just couldn't seem to settle down. She was still trying to make it as a singer, but she was past 30 now in a business that was more focused on young people. She claimed that the jazz music of her youth bored her, and she was mad about the vocal groups that seemed to be sprouting up in every neighborhood in Philadelphia.

At times she seemed younger than her son Pete. He was a serious boy who was obviously perplexed by his madcap mother. He seemed perpetually an outsider, someone who didn't fit in anywhere. And why wouldn't he feel that way? Most women Rosie's age were long married, not single mothers trying to raise a teenage son. Pete didn't know who his father was, which already made him different from the other boys he went to school with in 1960.

"You're not raising him right," Lucy would say to Rosie. "That boy needs a father, needs stability in his life. You haven't given him anything like that. He's looking for something to hold on to. You keep slipping through his fingers."

But Rosie didn't listen. She was always off on another adventure.

Lucy was walking along one day in 1960 when she saw a group of people near City Hall with picket signs. "Civil rights for the Negro now!" one of them said. "Desegregate the lunch counters down South!" another said. There was a man in his 40s with sandy hair, a gray shirt and a white clerical collar standing near them, making a plea for justice for Negroes in Nashville, where there were sit-ins going on at this very moment. He had a voice as mellow and rich as aged bourbon whiskey, and Lucy was transfixed by him.

"Who is he?" she asked a woman standing nearby. "He's the Reverend David Denton," the woman said. "He's organizing people to support the Nashville Sit-ins. They're trying to use peaceful means to desegregate the businesses in Nashville. Won't you join us?" she said.

And that was how Lucy got involved with something that gave her a cause, a reason for being.

From that day forward she went to meetings, picket lines, sit-ins, prayer services, demonstrations of every kind, and she dragged Paul along with her. "We must do something to fight this injustice. We must do something with our lives," she told him. Paul was hesitant at first, but he soldiered on, wanting to please her. He also felt enormous guilt about his wartime activities, she knew, and he was eager to do something to help people, to atone for what he'd done.

So the two of them became the grandparents of the local movement, always on the sidelines doing their part to help get justice for the Negro. Lucy became consumed with the task, and it seemed these impassioned young people were going to show

America a new way, a way to use peaceful means to overcome hatred and injustice.

And Reverend David Denton was such a shining figure to lead them! He seemed a gentle soul, a man of peace and Christian virtue, and Lucy was captivated by him. He spoke of how they had to love their oppressors, that love would help them reach their goal, that love was the only answer, etc. He was a hypnotic speaker, his voice cresting and peaking, now rolling back like the tide, now coming forward again with the same measured sweep of a tidal surge. It was relentless, and Lucy felt she could listen to him for hours.

Life was exhilarating again, and she loved it. She had not felt useful in so long, and all this activity helped her to push away the feelings of sadness, anger, and guilt that crept up on her sometimes. She was like a den mother for the earnest college students, helping to bandage their wounds when the police would hit them with nightsticks or throw them into paddy wagons to take them to jail for a night, counseling them in what to say to their worried parents when they were arrested, feeding them chicken soup when they got sick from picketing in cold, rainy weather.

Paul followed along like a loyal soldier behind her, never telling any of the college kids about his past, concentrating only on the present.

Rosie seemed interested in what they were doing, but she never stuck around long enough to get involved. She was too busy with whatever was happening in her life at the time.

Lucy started going to Quaker services, because the Quakers were very active in the movement. She liked the services where people would stand up and talk about their beliefs, saying what the

Spirit had moved them to say. She visited many churches, though, including David Denton's Episcopal church on 27th and Market Streets. There she heard him speak with power and elegance in his purple and black robes, standing at the carved oak podium that had been there for a hundred years, with the multicolored light from the stained glass windows falling on him like a rainbow. He looked like a man of God should look, with sandy long hair, clear blue eyes and a firm jaw. A leonine appearance, she thought.

It was all so idealistic, even ethereal, but Rosie brought her down to earth again, at least temporarily. In November of 1962 Rosie came to her and said, "Mom, I have to leave town for a while. I'm in trouble."

At first Lucy thought she was pregnant again.

"No," Rosie said. "I did something that got a very dangerous man angry."

They were sitting in Lucy's kitchen sipping mugs of tea, and Lucy could almost see the girl Rosie sipping her hot chocolate years ago after she'd come in from sledding, her eyes aglow with the excitement that came any time she did something risky.

"I shouldn't tell you," Rosie said. "But I had to do it. I don't care how tough he is, I had to get back at him for what he did."

"What are you talking about, dear?" Lucy said.

"It's some guy that I knew in South Philadelphia," Rosie said. "He's a bad character, and he hurt a boy I thought the world of. He ruined this boy's life, and I couldn't stand by and do nothing. I knew he was doing bad things, so I reported him. I'm not telling you any more than that, it's too dangerous. I just have to get away."

45

"But why?" Lucy said. "I still don't understand."

"Mom, this guy is a vengeful person, and I was told I needed to get out of town for awhile, to protect myself."

Lucy shook her head. "Rosie, I don't know about this life you're leading. You're leaving? Where are you going?"

"England," Rosie said. "Don't make that face, Mother. I know it's far, but I need to get far away. It will only be for a few years, then I'll come back."

CHAPTER SIX

1962

"Have you told Pete?" Lucy said.

"Yes, and he doesn't like it," Rosie said, looking down at her tea, as if it held the answer to her dilemma. He doesn't understand, and I can't tell him all the details. He's going to have to move in with you and Dad."

"Of course we'll take him in," Lucy said. "But he's only 16. What a time to make a young man change his life! He'll have to go to a new school, isn't that right? And in the middle of the school year!"

"Yes," Rosie said. "If he moves here, he has to go to West Philly high school. It means leaving his friends behind in the old neighborhood. There's no choice. I need him to lay low for awhile."

"But we're not that far away from where you live," Lucy said. "You can't really think that he'll be able to hide here. People will find him out."

"Oh, mother, you know how things are in this town," Rosie said. "The neighborhoods are like separate countries. If you go from one to another, it's like traveling to another time zone. Nobody from the old neighborhood will look him up here. Don't worry it'll be fine. He'll get used to it."

But he never did. Rosie moved the boy in to Lucy and Paul's house the next morning and left that afternoon. She had a cab waiting at the curb to take her to the airport, and she pulled Pete close and kissed him on the forehead and held him tight for a moment, then turned away with tears in her eyes and said, "Be good, Pete. I'll be back before you know it."

Lucy's heart almost broke to see the boy with his hands in his pockets, looking lost and alone as his mother drove off. She tried to comfort him, but he turned away and went upstairs to his room. He would not come out for a whole day, and when he did he seemed to have a hard shell of anger around him.

He went to the new school, but the very first day he got into a fight, and ended up with a broken nose and a missing tooth. It went on like that for the whole year, with Pete getting into scrapes, flunking tests, and breaking one rule or another. Lucy and Paul had regular appointments at the principal's office about him.

The principal, a stern woman named Mrs. Lennox, said, "But where are his parents?" the first time they showed up. They explained that his father was unknown to them and his mother was in England on business, and that she had to stay there for quite a while.

Mrs. Lennox did not seem to understand. "She should be here with her son," she sniffed. "He needs a mother. If this keeps up he's going to get in serious trouble."

Lucy felt terrible for the boy, and she tried to find something to cool his anger, something that he could hold onto. She tried to get him involved in the Civil Rights Movement with her, but he scoffed at it.

"Why do you want to get involved with all those Negroes?" he said. "They should stop trying to change things. There's nothing wrong with the way things are down South. People have lived the same way for years now; what's the point of trying to change it all?"

"But it's God's way," Lucy said. "God wants all men to be free. You should come with me and hear one of Dr. Denton's sermons about Civil Rights. It's so inspiring. It would change your life."

"Leave the boy alone," Paul would say, when he was alone with Lucy. "I know you're frustrated with him, but he's trying to handle a lot right now, and he'll come around. He's a good boy, and he'll see the light. You don't need to drag him to Dr. Denton's services; that won't work."

Indeed, Paul didn't seem to understand the power of Dr. Denton in Lucy's life. He seemed unmoved by the man's oratorical skills. Paul knew a thing or two about oratory, since he'd been a public speaker back in the 1940s. He told Lucy that Dr. Denton was just a good actor, that was all. "The difference is that he's using his acting skills for a good cause."

It made Lucy angry to hear Dr. Denton described as nothing more than an actor. She thought of him as the most purely good person she had ever met. The light of kindness and love simply radiated out from him. His wife Anna was always by his side, an adoring helpmeet if ever there was one, and his two tousle-headed blonde girls, 8 and 10 years old, came to all the demonstrations too. He was the most Christ like person Lucy had ever met.

He had a wonderful relationship with the black community, too. There was a man named Cicero Long, a black man from the South who had a law degree, and he was usually by Dr. Denton's side. He was a more fiery speaker, and he talked in the patois of urban blacks, his speech rough and ready, and on the edge of profane.

"We will not be denied," he would shout. "Our time has come, we are one, and we won't be denied by anyone."

Times were changing fast. With the election of John Kennedy, there was a mood of optimism. His brother Bobby was the Attorney General, and he seemed favorably disposed toward the Movement. There was a sense that after so many years of oppression, things were finally changing.

And then John Kennedy was assassinated. Lucy heard the news one morning when she was at Dr. Denton's church helping to stuff envelopes asking for donations for the legal fund. A woman rushed in and said, "The President's been shot. I just saw it on the news!"

The bottom seemed to drop out of everything. Lucy was glued to the television set for the rest of the week, trying to make sense of it all. She wept bitter tears watching the funeral, and seeing Kennedy's young son John saluting the color guard as they passed.

People seemed to get so much angrier after that. You could see it on their faces. The peaceful, measured tones, the sweetness and moral grandeur of Dr. Denton's sermons, was replaced by more strident tones. Bullhorns were at every rally, and speakers would use them to assault the listeners' ears with torrents of rage-filled rhetoric.

It carried over into every area of life. People seemed ready to argue, to fight, all the time. There were perceived threats everywhere, there were riots in the cities instead of peaceful marches, there was looting and burning and broken shop windows.

The nonviolent message of Dr. King seemed drowned out by the volume of the rage.

It carried into her own family. Pete took up boxing, and although Paul said it was probably a good thing, a way to vent his anger, Lucy didn't understand the urge to hit another human being, even for sport. It was foreign to her, this need for violence, and she fretted that Pete was going down a path of evil, rage, and immorality.

The world was speeding up. Rosie kept writing letters about this new musical group that was the talk of England, the Beatles, and when Lucy first saw them, sitting on her couch with Pete and Paul nearby, she had to admit they were fresh and young and upbeat. They had a new sound, something happy and joyful, and she thought it was a great relief from the anger and gloom, but Pete didn't like them at all. He was more set in his ways than an old person, and he didn't like change.

The boy was hurting so much, and Lucy didn't know what to do. He missed his mother terribly, and her monthly long distance calls were not enough to slake his loneliness and rage. She was always breathless on the phone, telling them about the many adventures she was having in the music business in London, which was becoming the center of the world, according to her. The phone line crackled with static, and sometimes her voice faded out, or the connection died altogether. It was so like Rosie, to fade out right in the middle of a good story.

CHAPTER SEVEN

November 1962

Rosie disembarked from a BOAC flight at Heathrow Airport in November of 1962, under a leaden sky that was spitting rain in horizontal sheets. She had arranged for Pete to live with her parents in West Philadelphia, 20 blocks away from her neighborhood in South Philly, which was like the other side of the world in a city divided into discrete neighborhoods like Philadelphia. If you were from South Philly in 1962 you didn't walk two blocks outside your neighborhood, so she felt Pete was as safe there as if he were in Patagonia.

In London she met the Dittybopper's friend, another fast-talking guy named Harry Helms, an American who was working at Capitol Records in the heart of the city. True to what the Dittybopper said, he got her a job as a secretary in the A&R department, and helped her find a visa and a flat in town with two English girls named Val and Diane.

The first night there she had her dream, the one where she was on a hillside running down toward the sweetest, most beautiful music she'd ever heard. This time there was something new, though, a jarring, jangly chord that kept repeating over and over. It was thrilling, and it made her blood jump with excitement. She raced down the hillside again, stumbling over her feet, and almost falling headfirst -- and then it was gone, once again. All was silence, with just the wind sighing in the trees.

Her two flat mates were merry girls who laughed a lot and were mad about some of the local bands. "You have to hear the

Beatles," Val said. "They're the latest thing, and everyone's mad about them."

"Oh, they're tired old wankers," Diane said. "Too nice for my taste. You have to see this group the Rolling Stones. They play every Sunday afternoon at the Crawdaddy club, and they're blues purists. They don't play that Everly Brothers pop, like the Beatles. They play Chicago Blues, and it's raw and rockin'!"

They took Rosie out the first week she was there, and from the first chords she heard from the stage of the Crawdaddy she felt like her world had changed. This was not the sweet harmony of the street corner groups of Philly, singing about true love and pledging their hearts to a girl. This was as black as the Deep South, a caterwauling, raw, hard-edged music about unfaithful women and back door men, and sometimes the notes weren't right but the energy, that raw energy was there to cover up for it.

Gypsy woman told my momma, before I was born/ You got a boy-child comin', gonna be a son-of-a-gun/ Gonna make these pretty women jump and shout/ And the world will only know, a-what it's all about.

(Hoochie Coochie Man)

She knew it was going to change everything. The kids at home were going to go for this in a big way, and the smooth as silk vocal groups would be dead as soon as the teens got a listen to this music.

And it wasn't just the sound. The band on stage had hair that came down past their ears, almost to the length of a girl's hairstyle in the States, and the singer wore tight pants and a loose white shirt, and he pouted his big red lips and put his hand on his hip and

53

paraded around with feminine movements, unlike any singer Rosie had ever seen before.

"Do you think they'll like it in America?" Val said, cupping her hand and shouting in Rosie's ear through the jangling guitars of "Little Red Rooster".

"I think they're going to go crazy for it," Rosie said, laughing with joy. "This group is going to be a sensation."

She would look back in later years and wonder about how right she was. Couldn't I have done more to tell people back in the States? She thought. It's like I saw a tidal wave coming before anybody else. I should have made them understand.

She did try, once, making a long distance call to the diner and getting the Dittybopper on the phone. "You have to listen, something big is about to happen," she shouted over the phone. "The music scene over here is about to burst."

"What's that you're sayin', darlin'?" he said, through a storm of static. "Did you say the music over there is the worst?"

It just didn't work. She couldn't make him understand. She hung up in frustration, but when she saw the headlines in the London newspapers a year later when the Beatles hit New York, she shook her head and knew exactly how it was going to turn out. She wrote a letter to Bobby Juliano and told him not to be too sad about his lost career, because his style of music was going to be dead in no time.

And it happened exactly that way.

To be young in London in the early 1960s was an exhilaration like no other. She knew she was old enough to be a big sister to these kids, but she looked and dressed younger than her age, and she jumped right into the scene with all the passion of an 18 year old. She went out every night to clubs, and within a month she knew all the bands, and could tell which ones were going to make it and which weren't. She became Harry Helms' assistant and she saw right away that he desperately needed help, he was fighting an uphill battle to convince his bosses in New York that something special was happening over here. With the success of the Beatles in England, the local record companies were in a frenzy to sign every English band they could. The folks back in New York, though, were skeptical about this English sound, and Harry was working hard to convince them, making transatlantic phone calls every other day, and spending his nights scouting bands all over the place.

Rosie's passion for the new sound got the better of her one day, and she strode into Harry's office and grabbed the phone out of his hand and told a very shocked record executive in New York that he was an idiot and he was going to regret the day he didn't sign some of these fresh new bands. "This music is going to wake everybody up over there, it's the most amazing thing to come along since jazz in the 1920s, and you're going to look like a fool for not recognizing that." She gave the phone back to Harry and walked out, convinced she was going to be fired. Instead, Harry said, "I need people like you. I'm fighting a lonely battle over here, and I need help."

So Rosie found herself taking the M1 highway up and down the spine of England, from the gray industrial cities of Leeds and Manchester to the gritty seaport of Liverpool, back to London, and even sometimes running over to Wales to hear some crooner who was supposed to sound like Elvis himself. Most of the time she was with Harry, but after awhile he trusted her judgment enough to send her out alone. He knew she wouldn't get carried away by a few long-haired boys with guitars posing on stage. He knew she would listen to see if they had something special, that ringing sound that would go right to a teenage girl's heart.

Things were moving fast, very fast, so fast that she barely noticed when President Kennedy got assassinated. She saw a headline in the London Times that was being hawked by a newsboy as she was waiting for a cab, and she paid him and read the story in the back seat, horrified, and got such a choking feeling of homesickness that she almost told the cabbie to take her straight to the airport to go home. Then she remembered she was due to meet with the Rolling Stones manager Andrew Oldham for lunch to get his ideas about any new bands she might want to hear. She knew it was only a matter of time before the Stones got very big, and she wouldn't have access like this forever.

She didn't go to the airport.

CHAPTER EIGHT

December 1963

Dear Pete,

I am sorry I haven't written much lately, but I have been so busy I hardly have time to eat or sleep. The music scene over here is just exploding, and I am right in the middle of it. London has clubs on every corner of some neighborhoods, and they're all packed with kids listening to sweaty bands playing loud guitar music. It's nothing like what we had at home, that sweet harmony singing with the vocal groups. I'm telling you, though, it's exciting and raw and it really connects with the kids. I think when these bands start coming over to America, the people over there are going to love them. Well, not the parents, of course. Even over here the parents don't like this music. There are stories almost every day in the newspapers about how this rock 'n roll is corrupting English youth. It doesn't make any difference -- the kids love it anyway. It's going to be huge, Pete, I'm telling you.

I'm so sorry about what happened to President Kennedy. I was shocked to read the news, and it made me feel sick to my stomach to think that could happen in my homeland. I remember how happy my grandmother Rose was when he was elected, the first Irish American Catholic President in history. What a proud day it was for her when she heard the election results! I think she finally felt like an American, she finally believed that our country really was a place where people could come and make something new of themselves. I hope the assassination had nothing to do with hatred of Catholics, the way some people are saying. It seems like the world is getting crazier all the time.

Your grandmother Lucy wrote to tell me you got in trouble again for fighting in school. Why does this keep happening, Pete? You used to be a good student, and now all I hear is how you're fighting, staying out late, and drinking. I know you miss having me around, but you know I had no choice, I had to leave. I got into some trouble last year and it was just better for both of us if we got out of South Philly. I wouldn't have done it if I didn't have to, Pete. It's not easy for me to be away from you, to talk to you only once a month on the phone, and to wait for your letters that never come. Thank God my mother writes regularly, otherwise I'd hardly know anything about what's going on in your life.

Grandma says you've been talking about going in the Army. I don't think that's a good idea. They might send you to a war, Pete, like that mess that's going on in Vietnam. I read in the newspapers that President Johnson might send more troops over there early in the new year. You don't want to get mixed up in that, do you?

My father fought in the First World War, and I think it did some damage to him. He certainly didn't behave well when the Second World War came along. Wars are destructive, evil things and I don't want to see you involved in one.

You're graduating from high school next June. Get a job somewhere, at a factory or maybe a garage, or someplace where you can work with your hands the way you like to. Find a girl to settle down with. Don't live the kind of crazy life I've had, always running after some new passion. I know my mother and father think I'm crazy, and maybe I am. I just haven't been able to settle down, although I know I should.

But, Pete, I feel so alive over here! It's a funny country in some ways, very proper and stiff upper lip and all that, but there's an undercurrent of pure passion here. I think these kids have been living in a box all their lives, and they want to break out. It's the way I feel sometimes, too -- like there has to be more to life than marrying and settling down.

I know, I'm talking out of both sides of my mouth. I'm telling you to have a settled life, but I'm saying that kind of life is not for me. I don't know, Pete -- if I knew the answer, I'd have had a much quieter time, wouldn't I? I'm just trying to figure it all out every day, and some days I think I've got it figured, but other days I'm just as lost and confused as when I was a little girl.

Your great-grandmother, my grandmother Rose, came from Ireland and she said her mother was touched in the head, but she always talked about another reality, another world that we couldn't see, we only got glimpses of it. She said her mother used to talk of spirits and fairy kingdoms, and she said there were beautiful realms around us, but most of us couldn't see them. Maybe that's the answer, Pete. Maybe there's another set of rules that we don't know about, an elaborate setup that governs everything. Maybe we'll get the answer some day, and it will all finally make sense.

Anyway, hang on, my darling boy. I pray for you every night, and I need you to please stay on the straight and narrow. Your grandparents are getting old, and they can't take it if you get them upset all the time.

I'm hoping to come back before too long. The Beatles, I've told you about them before, they're the most popular English band, and they're coming over in February to play on the Ed Sullivan show. I am convinced it's going to be a huge phenomenon, and there will be a demand for other English bands. If that happens, maybe I can hitch a ride with one of the ones I'm involved with. I sure hope

59

so. I miss you all terribly, even though I'm having the time of my life here.

Give my love to Grandma and Grandpa. Know that I love you and think about you always. And please don't live the way I've lived.

Love,

Your mom, Rosie

CHAPTER NINE

February 1964

"Look at the drummer!" Pete's grandfather said, pointing at the little television set from his easy chair. "That's no way to play the drums. He's holding the sticks wrong. I never saw anything so laughable." He had put down the newspaper he was reading so he could see for himself what all the fuss was about this English group called The Beatles, and he was not impressed.

"All those girls in the audience don't seem to mind," Pete's grandmother Lucy said. She was sitting next to Pete on the couch, and she seemed fascinated by the four long-haired boys on the screen. The music was tinny on the black and white TV set with the spindly rabbit ears, but the sound of hundreds of teenage girls screaming was like the steady roar of distant surf.

"And look at the hair on those fellows," Pete's grandfather Paul said. "What a strange collection of ragamuffins they are. I predict they won't last a week. American teenagers are too smart to be taken in by this English nonsense. Ed Sullivan will never have them back."

Pete didn't like them either. His mother had been writing him letters for months now about this group, telling him they were going to be a big hit when they came over to the U.S. She'd told him how they gave a command performance for the Queen, how they played sold out concerts all over Europe, how everyone under 21 couldn't get enough of their big beat and jangly guitars and edgy harmonies. "They're going to change the music scene," she'd gushed. "It's going to be big."

Pete didn't like change. He liked the street corner sound, the smooth harmonies, the sweet ballads and the finger popping up-tempo numbers like "Duke Of Earl". He listened to the Dittybopper's show all day long at the auto body shop, his little Japanese transistor radio on a shelf nearby, and he knew all the names of the local groups, as well as the ones from New York and Baltimore.

These long-haired guys in their collarless suits with their gawky stage movements were the enemy. They were what took his mother away from him.

No, he knew it wasn't really them. It was her, she'd done something stupid again. He didn't know the whole story, because his grandparents wouldn't tell him, but he guessed that she had shot her mouth off again, the way she always did. There were dangerous people in South Philly, he knew that, and his mother had crossed one of them somehow.

And because of that his whole life had turned upside down. He had to move in with his grandparents in West Philadelphia, finish his last year of high school at a different school, and be the only kid at graduation whose mother wasn't there. She wrote him letters which he never answered, and she called once a month, her voice fading in and out amid the static on the phone line, asking him why he kept getting into trouble.

He had no choice, the way he saw it. He had been the new guy in school, and the new guy had two options: either get beat up every day, or pick out the biggest guy on the football team and smash him in the mouth right upfront. He'd chosen the second course of action. He'd gotten his nose broken and a tooth knocked out from that fight, but it had established him as someone who would not back down. It also got him entry into a tough group of white kids known as the Runners, and although they protected him from then on, he had to join in their gang wars by default. There were bigger racial divisions here than in South Philly, and his gang often picked fights with the black gangs who maintained an uneasy presence in Thomas Jefferson High. He had been lucky to graduate high school at all, with all the trouble he'd gotten into for fighting.

As the Beatles finished their song and the camera cut to the screaming girls, some of them crying hysterically, Lucy smiled and said, "Oh, it's a wonderful thing to be that young and enthusiastic, isn't it? I think your mother is right about them, Pete. Those boys have talent."

"Humph," Paul said, rattling his newspaper in his easy chair. "It's nonsense. A lot of hullaballoo over nothing, just a bunch of long-haired clowns. It's a fad, that's all. Nobody will remember their names a year from now."

Pete clenched his bruised fists, running his fingers over the raised bumps and scars from his last fight. Lately, he'd been going to a gym where boxers trained. He'd gotten into the ring a couple of times for sparring sessions and done well enough to attract some interest from a trainer. The old man, Gappy Broadus, had told him he had potential, and put him on the bill for an amateur fight in a few weeks.

"What do you think, Pete?" Lucy said. "Do you think they're a fad? The young people seem to like them."

"Young people are stupid," Pete said, standing up. "I'm going out, grandma. Going for a run."

"What?" she said. "At this time of night?"

He leaned over and kissed her. "I have my first bout coming up in two weeks, remember? I'm in training. I'll see you later. Don't wait up for me."

He left, banging the door behind him as he went out.

Lucy shook her head. "I just can't get used to the fact that he's interested in boxing. It's such a violent sport. I don't understand the need to hit someone, don't understand it at all." She was doing a needlework picture that had a saying on it by Frederick Douglass, who was a hero of hers.

Paul nodded. "I know, but the boy seems to like it. I think it helps him to deal with the frustrations of his life, Lucy, and maybe it's helping him."

"I've tried to talk to him about Dr. King," Lucy said. "About non-violent principles. Violence only causes more violence, Paul, you know that. He won't listen to me, though."

"He's a boy," Paul said. "They're mostly all like that at his age. It's the rare one who doesn't enjoy bashing heads."

"Pastor Dave isn't like that," Lucy said. She went back to her needlework, concentrating furiously, her thin lips set in a hard angry line.

Paul sighed and went back to his newspaper. "I know, but we're not all saints like Pastor Dave," he mumbled.

CHAPTER TEN

October 22, 1962

Mercy Francis was sitting halfway down the length of Pan AM flight 230 to Philadelphia, with a notebook full of Nelson's instructions and a heart filled with trepidation. As she looked out the window of the plane she saw the landscape change from the mottled brown and tan of the desert to the flat yellow and green squares of the Midwestern farmland to the densely packed buildings of the mid-Atlantic, and finally the Philadelphia skyline came into view. It was dusk, and the fading sunlight from behind her bathed the city in a golden glow. She saw the statue of William Penn atop the City Hall building, and she remembered how her father had taken her to see it as a little girl, telling her that he had seen the workmen putting it together in sections at ground level and then raising it up with huge cranes to the top of the City Hall tower. "Why it was the most amazing thing, to get a heavy bronze statue like that to the top of the building," he said. "The things they can do in this country, my darling girl, are miraculous."

Her heart was pounding as the plane landed, and she wondered for the umpteenth time if she could pull this off. It had been 20 years since she'd been in the city, and she didn't know how she'd handle it.

When she collected her bag and walked outside the terminal all she knew was that she had a room reserved at the Barclay Hotel on Rittenhouse Square in the center of the city. It was an elegant, old hotel and very expensive, but Nelson had said, "I don't care how much it costs, you're staying there. You're on an important mission for me, and I don't want you living in some flea bag hotel. I have money to burn, darling, and I'd rather use it for this project than to buy another piece of sculpture for my living room."

She walked through the revolving doors and came out to fading, golden light, a chill that told her this was not Southern California anymore, and a line of yellow cabs with their drivers leaning against them, all of whom jumped to attention when they saw her, and came running over.

"Take your bags, Miss?" "Here, let me help you," "Where ya goin', lady?". They all crowded around her, and she was bewildered for a moment.

Then a voice cut through the noise like a knife. "Spread out, you guys. Give the lady some breathing room, will you?"

He was a compact man with wavy black hair and muscular forearms with black hair on them, and he carried himself with a gravity that made the other men back away. He had a blue Philadelphia A's baseball cap on, and a brown leather bomber jacket, and his smile showed rows of brilliant white teeth in an olive-skinned face.

"Good evening, ma'am," he said, taking off his hat and executing a deep bow. "Lorenzo Benedetto, at your service. I welcome you to our fair city, the city where this great country declared its independence from tyranny, and where freedom is still in the air." He took a deep breath, filling his lungs with air, and then letting it out. "Freedom!" he said. "It's the elixir of life!"

"Aw, don't listen to him," one of the cabbies said. "He talks like a college professor; he'll bore you to death."

"Yeah," another one said. "You get in Lorenzo's cab and you get to hear that crap for the whole ride. Come with me, pretty lady, and your ears will get a rest."

But there was something charming about this Lorenzo man, Mercy decided. He calmed her down after the emotional storms she had felt on landing in this city. His brown eyes looked kind, and she felt safe with him.

"Okay," she said, nodding to him. "I'll go with you."

"Excellent," he said. "Now, make way, gentlemen, for this beautiful lady." The other cabbies moved out of the way and Lorenzo took Mercy's suitcase and led the way to his yellow cab, waiting at the curb.

In the cab Lorenzo said, "Where to, my lady?" and when Mercy told him the Barclay Hotel, he said, "I would expect no less for such a classy and dignified lady as you. The Barclay is one of our oldest and most elegant hotels. You will enjoy your stay there."

Lorenzo had the radio tuned to a classical radio station, and he moved his hands in time to the music like a conductor. "That's the Philadelphia Orchestra," he said proudly. "It's the jewel of Philadelphia. One of the top three symphony orchestras in the world."

He was like a tour guide, although with a formal way of speaking. He kept up a nonstop commentary about the city and its history, pointing out landmarks, telling funny stories about neighborhoods they were driving through, mentioning the famous people who were buried in cemeteries they passed, recommending restaurants, and updating Mercy on local politics.

He also told her about his life. "I wasn't born here, you understand. I came here from Italy when I was just six, with my Mom and Pop. We're from Calabria, the hill country down around the toe of Italy. We moved here just after the First World War, when Italy was on the verge of collapse because of all the war dead and the country was close to bankruptcy. I remember how happy I was to get off the boat in this new country, where people wore shoes on their feet, and they all looked like they had plenty of food to eat. And it was a democracy, which meant rule by the people! Even as a boy I understood that was a good thing, instead of rule by the kings and queens like we had in Europe. This is truly a special country. Now, how about you? Were you born here?"

"Yes," she said. "I grew up in Philadelphia. We lived at 6th and Race streets, near Chinatown."

"Ah, Chinatown," Lorenzo said, nodding. "Now, that's exactly what I'm talking about. Those folks came here in the 19th century, looking for a better life. All these years later, people from China are still doing it. Do you know, there are more Chinese than ever moving into that neighborhood. Why, it's probably twice the size it was when you were a little girl."

"I wouldn't know," Mercy said. "I haven't been back in a long time. Twenty years."

Lorenzo whistled sharply. "Twenty years! That is a long time. Coming back to visit the relatives, are you?"

"No," Mercy said. "There's nobody left from my family. They're all gone. I'm just here on business, that's all."

"Business, eh?" he said. "Very interesting."

Mercy understood. He was having a hard time comprehending a woman who worked. He seemed to think it over for a moment, then he said: "If you don't mind me asking, what type of business are you in?"

"I work for an art dealer in California," she said.

"Art!" he said. "Now, that's a subject close to my heart. We have some amazing museums here in Philadelphia. The Museum of Art, of course, but there are others. Did you know there's one called the Barnes Foundation, and it has the best collection of Impressionist painting outside of Paris? Imagine that!"

"So you like art?" Mercy said.

"I'm in love with it," Lorenzo said. He touched the tips of his fingers to his mouth and then opened them, in the European manner. "Art is what makes Life worth living, don't you think? I could spend hours looking at paintings, sculpture. I go to the Barnes Foundation on my days off, and I take my lunch in a brown bag and I just sit there looking at those beautiful Impressionist paintings for hours. I love the way the changing light coming through the windows can make them look so different. That Claude Monet, he certainly was a master at capturing light. And Renoir, he painted such beautiful skin tones on his women. Beauty, that's something we can't live without, don't you think?"

"Yes, you're right," Mercy said. "But the world can be an ugly place sometimes." They happened to be passing through a neighborhood of looming brick factories and warehouses, their grimy brick facades like something out of a Dickens novel. Smoke billowed from their chimneys and the smell of it made Mercy's eyes water even inside the cab.

"It all depends on how you look at it," Lorenzo said. "The key is up here." He tapped his head with his finger. "I mean, you could see beauty or you could see ugliness, it just depends on how your brain processes things. Me, I see beauty."

Mercy chuckled. He certainly was different than the Philadelphians she remembered from her youth. They all seemed to walk around with their chins sticking out, ready for a fight. They were feisty, disagreeable sorts who never seemed happy unless they were in the middle of an argument. Her first husband had been like that, quick to take offense, and it had gotten him his nose bashed in twice and eventually got him killed in a bar fight. But that was long after Mercy had left him. That husband reminded her too much of the city where she grew up, and all she wanted to do at that point in her life was get away from it.

As Lorenzo drove on the sun set and the blanket of night fell on the city. The streetlights came on, and neon signs in store windows flashed their multicolored messages. People were going home from work, hurrying to the subway and the train station, and their faces showed a range of emotions.

"The evening is a special time, isn't it?" Lorenzo said. "Look at these people, all going somewhere. Have you ever stopped to think about all the people that will be sitting around the supper table tonight, regaling their loved ones with stories about what they did all day? It's amazing to think of that, isn't it?"

"Yes it is," Mercy said. "What about you?" she said. "Do you have someone waiting at home who wants to hear about your day?"

He was uncharacteristically silent for a moment, and then he cleared his throat and said, "Matter of fact, no. I never married, so I have no family. My Mom and Dad passed away a few years ago. I have a sister, but she lives in New Jersey. I'm what you call a confirmed bachelor, I guess."

"Oh," she said. She never knew what to say in these situations. I certainly have a talent for saying the wrong thing, she thought. Happens all the time.

Lorenzo regained his buoyancy very quickly, though. "How about you, ma'am? I know you're far from home, but you must have someone back there in California who's waiting to hear from you tonight."

"Actually, no," she said. "There's no one."

He stopped the cab in the middle of a block. "You must be kidding, right? A beautiful woman like you, without a husband? Why, that's a stunning fact, very hard to believe."

She looked down at her hands, bare of a wedding ring. She looked up and saw him looking at her through the rear view mirror. A car behind them started honking, and Lorenzo rolled the window down and said, "Keep your shirt on, buddy. I'm going." He put the cab in gear and started off again.

"I'm sorry," he said, after a moment. "I didn't mean to embarrass you. Lord, I'm always doing that, putting my foot in my mouth. I don't mean any harm, it's just, I thought someone as beautiful as you would have a husband." He slapped his palm to his forehead. "There I go again. I just can't keep my big mouth shut. I'll close my trap now, ma'am, don't worry. You won't hear a peep out of me anymore." He turned the dial on the radio, trying to find the classical station, but then a grim voice broke in:

"We interrupt this program to announce that President Kennedy is going to address the nation tonight on a matter of great importance. At 7:00 tonight the President will hold a news conference that will be televised live. Please tune in to your local station. Now, back to your regularly scheduled program."

Lorenzo whistled. "Ye gods, can you believe that? I bet it's about those Russian missiles in Cuba. It's been all over the news, and the situation seems to be getting worse. I think we all need to turn on the TV tonight and hear what President Kennedy has to say. Must be something very important."

He was silent for the next few minutes, until they got to the Barclay Hotel.

At the curb of the hotel a tall black doorman in a long maroon coat with gold braid and epaulets on the shoulders, and wearing white gloves, opened the door and helped Mercy out.

"Good evening, Madam," he said. "Welcome to the Barclay."

Lorenzo hopped out of the driver's seat and came around to the trunk, then opened it and got Mercy's suitcase out. The doorman seemed annoyed, as though the proper procedure was for him to do that.

"I'll take that inside," he said, grabbing the suitcase. He stood off to the side, waiting for Mercy to pay the cabbie.

"How much?" Mercy said to Lorenzo.

"Ten dollars," he said. "I wish I could have driven you for free, ma'am, for all the pleasure I got out of our conversation, but the cab company won't let me do that."

As she fished around in her purse for the money, he said: "By the way, if you need a cab at any time during your stay in our fair city, please keep me in mind. Lorenzo Benedetto, at your service." He took off his cap and did a sweeping bow, like he did at the airport.

She could not resist a smile. He was charming, there was no denying that, and he was interesting company.

"I might take you up on that," she said. "I need to go to the Museum of Art tomorrow, to meet with someone. Would you be available in the morning?"

His face lit up. "For you, ma'am, I will make myself available. Tomorrow is normally my day off, but I will gladly come in to work for you."

"That's very nice of you," she said. "Can you pick me up at 9:00?"

"I will be here at 9:00 sharp," he said. "I can't think of a better way to start my day than to see your beautiful face in the back of my cab."

"Oh, you talk such nonsense!" she said, laughing, as she handed him a ten dollar bill and a one dollar bill for a tip. "I must be very vain, to put up with all that flowery language, but anyway, see you at 9:00."

She turned to follow the doorman inside, but Lorenzo called after her. "Excuse me, ma'am, but I don't even know your name. I like to know my customers' names. Makes everything more personal, if you know what I mean. May I ask your name?"

"It's Mercy," she said. "Mercy Francis."

He smiled that radiant smile again, that seemed to light him up from inside. "Mercy. What a gorgeous name. I don't think I've ever heard that name before, but I'd say it fits you. You look as merciful as you are beautiful." He tipped his hat, bowed, and jumped back in his cab, then gunned the motor and was gone.

Mercy shook her head. What am I getting myself into? She thought.

CHAPTER ELEVEN

August 1964

"The blacks are crafty, good punchers, but they ain't got no heart," Gappy Broadus was saying. "If I hit 'em hard enough to make their eyes water, they go down like a house of cards, huh?"

Gappy was a wizened man with gaps in his mouth and a face like a leather coat that's been left outside all winter. He had wrinkles on top of his wrinkles, but he wouldn't say how old he was. Most of the boxers thought he was at least a hundred. He talked constantly, he always used the first person even when he was referring to one of his boxers, and his statements were always open to interpretation. He also liked to say, "huh" a lot, when he was prompting his fighters to agree with him.

He was wrapping Pete's hands in preparation for a bout against Schoolboy Johnson, a black fighter out of Pittsburgh, and tonight was Pete's third pro bout. They were in a dank, smelly dressing room in the bowels of the Civic Center, where there was a slate of fights scheduled every second Friday throughout the winter.

"Now this guy's been around a long time, so I got to watch out for him," Gappy said. "I can't do stupid things like I did in those amateur bouts." Here he tugged hard on Pete's laces, to make his point. "I was a dumb kid then, getting disqualified for hitting after the bell, huh?"

"Right," Pete said. "I won't do that again."

"I must always remember not to get angry," Gappy said. "Anger does me no good. Causes me to make mistakes, huh? Gets my thinking all bolloxed up. This Schoolboy Johnson fellow, he makes me pay if I get angry. Every time I get angry he puts a tattoo of his knuckles on my face, huh?"

"I know," Pete said. "Don't worry, I won't get angry." He was too nervous to get angry. He had a lot of friends in the audience, guys from the Runners, and some girls too. One girl in particular, her name was Darlene, he really wanted to impress her. He had had two dozen amateur bouts, but he got sick of the three rounders with all the padding and the headgear, and he wanted more action. He'd gotten disqualified a couple of times for stupid things like hitting after the bell, and he'd finally talked Gappy into letting him turn pro. His first two bouts were easy wins, and now he was getting a chance at someone better. Johnson was a seasoned veteran on the downside of his career, but he still commanded a measure of respect from the fight crowd. A win tonight and Pete would be on his way.

He'd invited his grandparents, but he knew they probably wouldn't show up. His grandmother had turned pacifist and kept preaching all this nonviolent garbage, and they were both active in the Civil Rights Movement, always running off to some demonstration or rally somewhere. He didn't understand them at all. Life was all about fighting, the way Pete saw it. You either lowered the boom on someone, or someone was going to lower the boom on you. Either way, it wasn't a peaceful world.

"All right, it's time for me to get out there," Gappy said. He put a red terry cloth robe around Pete's shoulders and guided him out the door into the hallway, and Pete was immediately hit by the smell of cigars and beer. They walked through a narrow cement hallway toward an opening about fifty feet away, where they could hear the echoing noise of the crowd. They came out at the lower level of the arena, and Gappy led Pete down past ten rows of seats to get to the ring. This was the first bout of the night, and the place was still filling up. Pete saw his crowd sitting in the front row, and he felt a thrill to see Darlene blow him a kiss. She was a dark-haired beauty with cobalt blue eyes, and he wanted nothing more than to impress her tonight.

Gappy helped him through the ropes, and he got his first glimpse of Schoolboy Johnson. The black man was tall, with exceptionally long arms. His muscles were not well defined, and he had a little paunch hanging over the waistband of his white trunks. His face was scarred, with a broad, flat nose that looked like it had been broken several times. He stared at Pete impassively, as if he were looking at a job of work he had to finish so he could go out and have a beer.

Gappy was talking to him, but Pete found it hard to listen. The old man talked constantly, and although he certainly had nuggets of wisdom to impart, it sometimes seemed like too much effort to pick them out of the background noise of his conversation.

Just stay away from those arms, Pete told himself. Go inside and whack away at his body, hit that soft belly and the ribs hard. Then, when he gets tired of all those body shots and starts dropping his hands, hit him on the jaw with your left, and it'll all be over.

It was time for the instructions, and Gappy led him to the center of the ring, where the referee, a no-nonsense man with a steel gray crew-cut and an expression like he was sucking on a lemon, gave them the rundown.

Pete stared at Schoolboy, who was still looking at him like he was of no more consequence than a fly in his soup. His hooded eyes were half-closed, as if he was ready to doze off. "You're in for a big surprise," Pete said, just loud enough for the black man to hear. "You ain't never been in the ring with a puncher like me."

Johnson betrayed no emotion at that comment; he just kept staring at Pete. When the referee told them to "shake hands and come out fighting," however, he took Pete's hand with both his gloved hands and broke into a smile. "It's nice meeting you," he said. "I'm sorry about what I have to do to you tonight." He turned and walked back to his corner before Pete could answer.

"The black man tries to get inside my head," Gappy was saying, back at Pete's corner, "but I will not let him. I am too smart for that."

But Pete couldn't stop thinking about what Johnson had said. It was annoying that this broken down old fighter was treating him like a child. It was disrespectful. I'll show him, Pete thought. I'll knock him on his ass, and then we'll see who's the one getting the respect.

The bell rang and Pete came out swinging. He missed the first three punches in a row, as Johnson deftly sidestepped and connected with Pete's jaw as he lunged forward. The punches were not hard, and Pete shrugged them off.

"That ain't nothing," he said, through his mouthpiece. "My grandmother hits harder than that."

Johnson didn't say a word, but instead he peppered Pete with two hard left jabs that made his eyes water. Pete lunged again, but this time Johnson tied him up with those long arms. It was like getting tangled up with an octopus, and Pete struggled to get free.

"I'm sorry, young man, for what I have to do to you," he said, through his mouthpiece, just before the referee broke them apart.

His condescending tone of voice was maddening, and it only made Pete more determined to make him pay. He swung with all his might at the black man's soft belly, hanging there like a target, but he only landed one punch for every three he took, and Johnson was so adept at moving his body that the punches only glanced off his stomach, never connecting with any real force. And every time Pete missed, he got stung with another counter punch that connected with his jaw, his, chest, or his ribs.

By the time he went back to his corner at the end of the round his head was spinning and his jaw was throbbing. The black man's punches were not hard one at a time, but collectively they took a toll.

"I am making a lot of mistakes out there," Gappy said, as Pete drank from the water bottle. "I am letting my emotions get the better of me, huh? I cannot get angry and make mistakes. This is a chess match. If I try to slug it out with this man I will get hurt. I must be a man of reason out there, huh?"

"He's making a fool of me, in front of my friends," Pete said. "Nobody does that. I'm going to make him pay."

Gappy grabbed his chin and brought his face nose to nose with Pete. "Listen to me, young man. I cannot throw the right hand wildly like that--"

"Stop saying, 'I', dammit!" Pete said. "You aren't the one getting hit, Gappy, I am."

79

The old man stared at Pete, his face wrinkling in frustration, and then he sighed. "Go," he said, pushing Pete out of his seat as the bell rang for Round Two. "Have a ball out there, young man."

Round Two was more of the same. Pete wanted nothing more than to get close enough to tag the black man hard, to break his ribs with some hard body shots. He never seemed to be able to get there, though. He was always off balance, missing, swinging at a phantom that disappeared before his fist got there. And every time he missed he got tagged with another punch, another stinging shot that made his face throb and his energy sag. In the clinches, when Johnson wrapped him up with the skill of a wrestler immobilizing his opponent, the black man was apologetic. "Sorry, son, don't worry, it'll be over soon. You doin' a good job, just need more fights, that's all."

Pete could hear the frustration in his friends' voices, in the seats below the ring. "Come on, Pete," they were yelling. "What's the matter? Hit that old man, will you? Put him down!" Darlene's voice was among them, and the note of disappointment in her voice was what goaded him the most.

He wasn't going to let this happen. He wrestled the black man around the ring, shouting, "Let me go, you coward. You're a yellow belly, that's all. Fight me like a man, will you?"

The referee broke them apart again, and Pete swung a roundhouse right, desperate to make contact with Johnson's midsection.

The next thing he knew he was on the canvas, and his head was throbbing again. His vision swam and he heard the referee counting, "1. . .2. . .3. . .". He got up on one knee, then saw the rope was nearby, so he grabbed it and pulled himself up. The referee had just counted "8", but Pete started bouncing on his toes, trying to show that he was ready to fight again. Johnson was standing in his corner looking like he wanted it to end. "Come on," Pete said. "Let's go. I'm ready."

But then the referee waved his hands and shook his head. "This fight is over," he said. "Go back to your corner."

"What do you mean?" Pete said. "I'm not quitting. I'm ready to go. You can't stop this fight."

"Yes I can," the referee said. "Your corner just threw in the towel."

Pete turned to see Gappy climbing through the ropes, and the old man was shaking his head. "The evening is finished," he was saying. "Time to go home, young man."

"You can't do that!" Pete said. "I'm still good. I can beat him. I'm just getting warmed up. It's not fair!"

Johnson was already gone, halfway to his dressing room, and Pete could see the corner men for the next bout setting up in his corner. Pete's friends were booing, but otherwise the crowd was silent. They were already looking forward to the next bout on the card.

Gappy put his hands on Pete's shoulders. His gnome like face was close to Pete's and his flinty gray eyes looked surprisingly kind and gentle in the harsh overhead lights.

"You did your best, son," he said. "Now it's time to go home. Go home, go get a malted or a root beer float, or maybe a nice cup of tea, and relax. You'll feel sore tomorrow, but in a couple of days you'll forget this little incident, huh?"

He led Pete through the ropes, past his now silent friends, and down the runway to the dressing room. Pete knew he wouldn't sleep tonight.

CHAPTER TWELVE

April 1965

Lucy refused to go to Pete's boxing matches, but Paul went to a few of them, just to make sure he was all right. The night that Pete's career ended, that was etched in Lucy's mind forever. She would never forget the sadness on Paul's face as he came through the door before Pete, and the way Pete looked when he came in afterward. It was not so much his swollen, discolored face that shook Lucy up, it was the lost look in his eyes. He had thought he could have a career, a purpose, in boxing, but this night he had had his dreams shattered by a boxer who was vastly better than him, and he didn't know how to replace the broken dreams. He looked utterly lost and utterly alone.

He stayed that way for a while, but then he came home one day six months later and said he'd enlisted in the Army. "Whatever for?" Lucy shrieked, standing at the sink. She dropped a plate on the floor and it shattered into a hundred pieces, and she felt like it could have been her heart.

"It's an unjust war," Lucy said. "President Johnson is sending troops over there against the will of the people. Nobody supports this war. We're killing innocent people to further a policy that's morally wrong. Why would you want to join the Army and be part of that?"

"It's the patriotic thing to do," Pete said. "This is a great country, and I want be a part of the military."

"Patriotism is a smokescreen," Lucy said. "They use that word to brainwash young people into doing what they want. Don't you see? This isn't a war like the Second World War, where there was a clear evil. This is a morally ambiguous conflict, and there are serious questions about whether we should even be there. I don't want to see you go halfway around the world and get killed or maimed for this phony war."

But Pete was nothing if not stubborn. He stuck his chin out like he used to when he was a little boy and he said, "I'm going. It's the right thing to do, Grandma. Don't try to talk me out of it."

Lucy was distraught, and so was Rosie, when Pete told her the next time she called. Lucy could hear her shrieking at him on the phone, telling him not to do it. "Come over here!" she shouted. "I'll find you a job. You can live with me, just like old times. I forbid you to do this!"

"No," Pete said. "You can't tell me what to do anymore. You may not realize it, but I'm all grown up now. I can do what I want." He hung up the phone in the kitchen with a clang, and stormed up to his room.

Rosie called back in five minutes, but he wouldn't come to the phone. She wept bitter tears to Lucy, wailing that she was going to lose her son. Lucy wanted to tell her that she had been losing him for years, but what good would that do? She asked once again if Rosie could come home, but Rosie said it was still too soon, she couldn't risk coming back to the States yet.

Lucy hung up the phone with a sinking feeling. She felt like her family was falling apart, and there was nothing she could do to prevent it.

When Pete went off to Basic Training she wept the whole night afterward, and she realized she hadn't felt this kind of grief since her baby girl died so long ago in the 1920s. It was harrowing, soul-wrenching, and she almost felt that kind of desperate sadness that she had felt as a young woman. Then it was her mother-in-law Rose who had pulled her out of it, spoken to her in a clear, strong voice and told her to get up and keep moving forward, it was the only thing to do. She remembered that voice, how it cut through the fog of her sadness, and it brought her solace now.

Just move forward, that is all.

So she did. She got even more active in the Movement, and now her passion for Civil Rights was fused, like so many other people's, with the Anti-War Movement. She picketed, she marched, she took buses to Washington and handed out leaflets in front of the White House, she raised funds, she cooked, she listened to innumerable speeches.

Paul tagged along, but his Parkinson's was getting worse, and now his head shook sometimes, along with his hands. He was a wispy, thin figure by her side, nodding off during the speeches, holding her hand to steady himself at times, trying to make jokes about his faltering powers.

She was still in good health, and in her secret heart she was impatient with the way his body was giving out. She did not want this, did not want to be his caretaker now, not when there was so much happening outside in the world. She had raised their children when he was away, as he first built his career and then wrecked it with his crazy Nazi infatuation, and she was the one who cleaned up all the messes, she was the one who suffered most when he came crashing to earth. She had endured so much, and this was finally, finally her time! It was unfair that she had this elderly man dragging her down, so unfair.

And Paul was no match for Dr. Denton in her fantasies now. Dr. Denton was in the prime of his life, a man of 50, with gravitas and moral weight in every fiber of his being. He still preached nonviolence, but he did it with wit and an orotund speaking style that mesmerized audiences. He was a darling of the Movement, and he attracted followers like a magnet.

Many of them were young, idealistic college girls, and Lucy saw how they followed him like he was a rock star. She thought it was harmless; they were simply hero-worshipping him, although she noticed that his eye seemed to have a bigger gleam in it when girls like that were around. She resented them for their youth and beauty, but she knew that if she were their age she'd be in their shoes, following him around and hanging on his every word.

CHAPTER THIRTEEN

February 1968

The rain was coming down in sheets and Pete huddled by the window of the house, soaked to the skin, water dripping down the back of his neck, his fatigues plastered to his body in the thick, humid air.

"Man, you got a smoke?" the black kid next to him said. They had been fighting house to house in the Vietnamese city of Hue for the past two days, and they had both come together only a minute ago from different directions to find shelter from the rain and sniper fire in this bombed out shell of a house. It had obviously been rocked by bombs, and a palm tree had fallen through the roof. The front door was missing, and the place seemed ready to collapse at any moment. There was enough shelter in the front room, where both soldiers lay sprawled among debris on the floor, so that they were dry and protected long enough to catch their breath.

Pete didn't normally talk to the black soldiers. It wasn't that he didn't like them, but there were sharp divisions between blacks and whites in his neighborhood at home, and he knew which side he was on.

The kid looked scared out of his wits, though, and Pete felt sorry for him. He reached in his jacket pocket and pulled out a wet pack of Camels. There were two left. He took one for himself, and then threw the pack to the other soldier, who took out the last cigarette, put it in his mouth, produced a shiny silver lighter from his pocket, flicked it and lit his cigarette, then held it close to Pete's so he could light it.

"Thanks," he said, exhaling smoke in a stream. "Damn, I needed that. Ain't had a smoke all morning. I lost my stuff in a mortar attack first thing today. Blew up most of my squad. We were in a square just south of here, out in the open. I had to scramble my ass to get out of there, and I dropped everything and just ran. Lost everything but my gun and my lighter. Can't lose that lighter, my girl gave me that."

Pete knew the kid was just jabbering out of fright. He'd seen that a lot in soldiers this last 18 months. Fear did strange things to people. Some guys clammed up, some got a haunted look in their eyes, some lashed out, and some could not stop talking no matter how much they tried. Pete just tried to stifle it, keep the panic out of his mind, ignore the screaming in his gut. It always came back at night, in his dreams, but at least he could keep it at bay when he was awake.

"You got a girl?" the boy said. He looked much younger than Pete, like he was barely past puberty, with big wide eyes and a head that seemed too large for his body. He looked like he was at that awkward age when his body hadn't finished its growth spurt, and his torso needed to catch up to his head.

"Not right now," Pete said. "I'm between girlfriends."

"That's a shame. Best thing that ever happened to me, meeting Peaches."

"Peaches? That's her name?"

"Naw. I just call her that. Her name is Betty Taylor, but I don't like that name. I decided to call her Peaches. She's a sweet thing, just like peaches and cream. I think about her all the time. She's the only thing that helps me get through this craziness."

Just then a burst of gunfire erupted from nearby, and there was the sound of bullets pinging off metal surfaces and thudding into the wall of the house. They put their heads down against the floor till the gunfire stopped.

"Damn, I hate this," the boy said. "I hate this so much. I only been here two weeks. Just my luck, I get sent over here in time for the biggest damn Viet Cong offensive of the war. Man, I want to go home. Don't you want to go home? Where you from?"

"Philly," Pete said.

"Me too," the boy said, sitting up again. "North Philly. Right near 23rd and Columbia, where the riots was a few years ago. Man, I thought I lived in a dangerous place, but it wasn't nothing compared to this. If I ever get home again, I'm going to park my ass in church every Sunday. My Daddy's a deacon in the first Holiness United Savior Church, and my Mama sings in the choir. I know they're praying for me right now. You got family at home?"

"Just my grandparents," Pete said. "They're pretty old. My mother lives in England."

"England! Damn, that's far away. What's she doing over there?"

"She works in the music business," Pete said. "I don't know too much about what she does. She's been gone a long time."

"You write to her?"

"I'm not much of a letter writer."

"You should write to her. She's probably worried about you. I write home a lot. I got two letters on me right now, one to Peaches and one to my Mama. I'll mail them as soon as we get out of this mess."

Just then there was more gunfire, and a soldier came leaping through the front door, tumbling along the floor till he got out of the line of fire. He was a sergeant, with a three day growth of beard and the glow of combat in his eyes.

"What are you guys doing in here?" he said, crouching between them.

"Just taking cover, sir," Pete said. "We've been fighting all morning, and--"

"And you're not finished," the sergeant growled. "There's no time for cigarette breaks. This area is not secure. There are gooks in the hotel down the street, that's where the firing is coming from. There's a unit of our men three houses up, on this side, a place with pink shutters. Follow me up there, and we will plan a course of action."

"But sergeant," the black kid said. "I'm all in, I've been fighting all morning, and my unit got blowed up three streets over. I lost all my stuff, and--"

"Shut up," the sergeant said. "What do you want, a free trip home? This is a war, soldier, and it's either kill or be killed. You're over here to do a job, now get your ass up and follow me."

Pete saw the look of abject fear in the boy's eyes. "Maybe he should stay here," he said to the sergeant. "He could meet up with us later."

The sergeant turned on him like a caged animal. "What are you smoking, private? Nobody stays in this house alone. You're surrounded by gooks, and it's only a matter of time before they show up on the doorstep. This is no safe place. Now, follow me -- that's an order!"

He crawled on his belly to the doorway, then said, "Come on!" and scurried half crouching out the opening, firing away as he made for the doorway down the street.

"Come on," Pete said. "You heard him. Let's go!"

"What's your name?" the boy said, grabbing Pete's arm. "Mine's Luther. What's your name?"

"It's Pete. Let's go!" Pete said. He bolted out of the doorway, following the sergeant. He heard bursts of fire, and he ducked involuntarily, cursing himself for showing fear. Behind him he heard Luther shouting as he ran.

"Yaaaa!" he was saying. "You ain't going to kill Luther Copeland! No sir, ain't nobody going to kill Luther Cope--"

And then there was a thudding sound and the splash of a body falling in the muddy street.

Pete had his back plastered against a doorway 25 yards ahead, and he turned to see Luther lying face down in the mud, his legs twitching. The sergeant was one house away, waving Pete forward. The next house up from him was the house with the pink shutters.

"Sergeant, we have a man down," Pete shouted.

"Leave him," the sergeant said. "You can't risk it. Get up here with me, we have to get to the next house."

Pete hesitated. Luther's legs were still twitching. There was blood pooling in the gutter next to him.

"Get up here, soldier," the sergeant bellowed. "That's an order!"

Pete bolted back toward Luther, staying close to the houses till he got to Luther's body, then flopped down in the mud and crawled forward. He could hear the sergeant yelling at him, but he ignored it.

When he got to Luther he turned him over, and he saw immediately that he was gone. His big eyes were staring nowhere, the look of fear still covering his face. The sergeant was roaring for him to run, and now there was a burst of gunfire, and bullets splashed into the puddles all around Luther's body.

The letters. It somehow became very important to get the letters. He rifled through Luther's bloody fatigues, and found a lump of something in his pants pocket. It was a clear plastic bag with two white envelopes inside it. He stuffed them in his pants pocket as bullets kicked up water all around him, and the sergeant continued to bellow something about insubordination. He was about to leave when he remembered the lighter. He reached into Luther's bloody shirt pocket and found the silver lighter, then stuffed it in his pocket with the envelopes.

Bullets were flying all around him, some thudding into the tree trunks, others hitting the walls of the houses. A large palm branch fell at his feet, its leaves fluttering like ostrich feathers. He put his head down and half crawled, half ran toward the sergeant, who was firing furiously into a house across the street to cover him. When he got to the sergeant, the other man barked, "Stupid move, Private. You could have been killed. Now, follow me, and make it snappy."

They scrambled down the street, with gunfire popping all around them, and Pete could see GIs firing from the windows of the house with the pink shutters. There was a side door that was open, and a soldier with an ammunition bandolier crisscrossed on his torso waving them forward. Pete and the sergeant stumbled and tripped along the muddy ground the last few yards, then dove through the doorway and fell on their faces on the tile floor.

CHAPTER FOURTEEN

October 22, 1962

Inside the Barclay Hotel Mercy quickly noticed there was something troubling going on in a room just off the lobby. There was the sound of a TV, and she could see people huddled around a huge black and white set with rabbit ears on top of it. The volume was turned up very loud, and Mercy could hear President Kennedy's voice, the broad Massachusetts accent, the clipped cadences. He sounded very serious, even grim. After she checked in at the front desk she walked over to the TV room and stood at the back and watched.

It took a while for her to figure out what he was talking about, but the gist of it seemed to be that the Russians had secretly installed missiles in Cuba, and Kennedy said it was an act of aggression that could not be tolerated.

Kennedy's grim face without its characteristic wry smile, and the eyes of the people in the room told Mercy the other part of the story, that these were nuclear missiles. With atomic bomb warheads.

She heard isolated words and phrases, "unmistakable evidence", "nuclear strike capability", "crisis", "explicit threat", "sovereignty of our boundaries", "arms buildup", "plea to Premier Krushchev", and the like, but there was a slow, sinking feeling that this was serious business.

Kennedy seemed to age as the speech went on. His voice seemed shrill and tense, his face looked haggard. The silence among the group around the television set crackled with tension.

When he finished his address, saying, "Thank you, and good night," someone switched off the TV set and there was a moment of grim silence, when the weight of his words seemed to sink in. Then a woman sitting near the TV started sobbing softly, and when the man next to her whispered something in her ear to comfort her, she said, "But I don't want to die, Harry."

She did not shout or scream, it was just a simple statement in a trembling voice, and it cut like a knife. Mercy realized that everyone in the room was thinking the same thing: that they could all go to bed tonight and not wake up in the morning, that the horror of atomic war was suddenly very real to them.

Later, in her hotel room, she called Nelson. It was evening in California, and he said he had watched Kennedy's address also.

"I'm sitting here watching the sunset," he said, his voice betraying a slight tremor. "I'm wondering if it will be the last one I ever see. Oh, well, I guess I shouldn't complain. I'm dying anyway, so what's the difference if I waste away from cancer or get burned to a crisp from an A bomb?"

"Nelson, you're not at risk," she said. "The missiles in Cuba can't reach you. I'm the one who could get burned to a crisp."

"Okay, technically you're right," he said. "But if things get to the point where we're lobbing missiles at each other, I don't think anybody is safe. I'm sure they have missiles somewhere in Russia that could land in my backyard."

"This is scary," Mercy said.

"Well, say your prayers," Nelson said. "I hope you don't have any regrets in your life, darling."

95

Mercy was silent. Regrets? She had many, for sure. All those mistakes she'd made with men, the great train wreck she'd made of her love life, always picking the wrong men to marry. Had she ever truly been in love? She couldn't say.

As if he read her mind, Nelson said: "Have you had love in your life, darling? You know, I think that's the key. If you can look back and say you loved and were loved in return, then it was a pretty good run. I can say it, thankfully, even with all the drama. Can you?"

"Oh, I suppose so," she said. "I think I have. I mean, I guess so. Oh, how can we know something like that, Nelson? It's so hard to know if you've ever truly--"

"Darling, listen to me," he said. "You know. It's that simple."

She was silent, unable to speak. She knew Nelson was waiting for an answer, but she couldn't give it.

"Well, I love you," Nelson said. "You should know that before we get bombed into the Stone Age. I love you very much. I would marry you, except that I'm not the marrying kind."

She laughed. "I know that, Nelson. And I know you love me, so that makes my life complete."

"Of course it does," he said. "Anyone would be happy to have Mr. Nelson Parnell love them. I mean, I'm Hollywood. Old Hollywood. I'm an icon. I know the kids today don't know me, but Baby, my name was up in lights at one time. I had fan clubs. I had teenage girls swooning over me. A fat lot of good it did me, of course, since I wasn't inclined in that direction, but anyway, I did have my moment of glory."

"I know," she said. "You're a part of old Hollywood, aren't you?"

"You don't have to mention the 'old' part," he said. "Although that's why I want you to find those reels with my stellar performances for Mr. Lubin. I want to look at them one more time and remember what it was like to be 19 years old and starting out in life, taking those first baby steps toward my destiny. God, I felt like a comer back then, a beautiful boy with the whole world in front of me and people just starting to notice that I was someone to watch."

"My God, Nelson," Mercy said. "I've always known you had a big ego, but it's really exploding tonight. Have you had too much wine?"

"No," he said. "Not even one glass. All this nuclear war talk is making me crazy, I guess."

"Well, it's late here," Mercy said. "I need to get to bed. I don't care if I might not wake up tomorrow, I'm tired and I need my sleep."

"Okay, sweet dreams," he said. "And if we don't wake up tomorrow, I'll see you in Heaven, darling."

"Right," she said. "Like St. Peter is going to let you in Heaven. Good night, Nelson."

She dreamed many dreams that night, but the one that seemed most vivid had Lorenzo in it. His broad smile, the creases around his eyes that bespoke gentleness, his muscular arms, his

97

compact body, the musical cadences of his voice. He was there in her dreams, pointing the way to someplace wonderful, pointing down a garden path that promised to hold many wonders just around the bend, on the other side of some azalea bushes.

CHAPTER FIFTEEN

November 1967

Rosie was wearing white go go boots and a skirt that was so short it barely covered her bottom, and she was walking down Carnaby Street feeling as frisky as a 17 year old, and knowing she looked almost as good. She was with Harry Helms, who was dressed in a full-length red velvet cape, psychedelic sunglasses, and flowered pants, and he was smoking a cigarette in a gold holder. They were on their way to see an American guitarist who was sparking some excitement in London. He played in the new psychedelic style that had swept over the Atlantic like a tsunami, and everybody wanted to hear him in person.

Harry was not with the record company anymore. He had his own management agency, and he had a stable of some of the hottest bands in England. Rosie was his secretary, Girl Friday, assistant, and he counted on her to help him stay ahead of the curve, to find the next New Thing that would take over the entertainment world.

They passed a pub, and a group of men came out. It was a place called the Crown and Shield, an old stodgy place that seemed out of place here in the heart of Swinging London. Rosie was chatting with Helms and not paying attention to what was in front of her, when she stumbled on a pebble on the sidewalk and fell headfirst.

She was inches from the ground when a pair of strong arms seemed to come out of nowhere and grab her. They pulled her up, and she heard a familiar voice say, "Caught you! It's worth your life to walk about in London these days, isn't it?"

She knew that voice, although she hadn't heard it in more than 20 years.

"Charlesworth," she said, looking at the slim man with gray hair and a network of lines around his steel blue eyes who was holding her. "James Charlesworth, right?"

At first he didn't recognize her, but then it was like a light went on in his eyes. "Rosie? Is that you?"

"The one and only," she said, pushing away from him. "Nice to see you again, James."

He looked flabbergasted. He moved his lips, but no sound came out. If it weren't evening Rosie thought she would have been able to see him blushing.

"Who's your friend, James?" a man in the group said.

"Ah, uh, my friend is. . . my friend is--"

"Rosie Morley," Rosie said, sticking out her hand. "Pleased to meet you." She knew that the reserved English did not really like shaking hands, but sometimes she did it just to unnerve them. This was one of those times.

"Right," the other man said, frowning uncomfortably. "A Yank, are you? James, I didn't know you had friends of the American persuasion."

He was a toff, a man of the upper crust, and from the looks of it, so were James' other companions. Rosie loved toying with men like that.

"Oh, James has lots of American friends, don't you James?" she said, coyly. "Actually, we go way back. I knew James during the war, isn't that right, honey?"

He looked extremely embarrassed. "Ah, yes, I believe we did know each other a bit."

"Nonsense," one of the other men said. "This girl looks like she wasn't even born back then."

"Why thank you," Rosie said, smiling. "I appreciate that. But, unfortunately, it's true. I'm older than I look, sadly."

There was an awkward silence, while James struggled to find something to say.

"Well, I'm sure it's been nice to see an old acquaintance," Harry said, "but we have places to be, Rosie. Say goodbye to your friends."

"Goodbye," Rosie said. "Nice meeting you, gents. And look me up sometime, James. Aquarius Talent Management. Number 16, Bond Street. Bye!"

She kissed James on the cheek, just to deepen his embarrassment, and walked off laughing with Harry.

"What was that about?" Harry said, when they were out of earshot. "You sure embarrassed that bloke. And I can tell you're pretty wound up yourself. You're shaking like a leaf."

It was true, Rosie's legs were shaking so much she had to hold onto Harry with a death grip just to avoid falling.

"Who is he, an old boyfriend?" Harry said.

"I guess you could say that," Rosie replied. "I, ah, used to be in love with him. A long time ago."

Harry was aghast. "That tight ass? He doesn't seem like your type. And I thought you were never in England before you came over five years ago. How did you meet him?"

They were waiting at a traffic light, the pavement crowded with people getting out of work, and some early theatergoers. Rosie paused until the light changed. She was having a difficult time pulling her thoughts together.

"I met him during the war," she said. "He was in the Royal Navy, and he was sent over on official business to the Philadelphia Navy Yard. I was singing at the USO and he came in one night. I liked him from the start. It all just mushroomed from there."

"A wartime romance, huh?" Harry said. "Love 'em and leave 'em, right Rosie?"

"That's right," she said. She tried to be blasé about it, but suddenly the bottom had dropped out of her day. She felt sad, beaten, lost, with a big void inside her. She pulled her puffy Afghan coat closer around her, suddenly cold.

"Are you okay?" Harry said. "You don't look well, all of a sudden. You want to skip this little outing, go get a cup of tea somewhere? We can see this guitarist another time. He's playing all over town, you know. And he's probably all hype anyway. I heard he was playing on the chitlin' circuit down South just a year or two ago, as a backup guitarist. How good could he be?"

"Don't worry about me," Rosie said, suddenly straightening up. "I don't need tea. What I need now is some loud guitar music. Really loud. Come on!"

She tried to drown out the feelings with loud music in yet another cramped sweaty little club. The American was amazing, a breathtaking, extravagantly talented guitarist who played at ear-splitting volume. He was like a Martian who played the blues -- the notes were all there, but they were turned upside down and inside out, like he was examining each one as he played it.

She drank too much, smoked some killer weed, and ended up debating philosophy with some guitarist she couldn't keep in focus in the back seat of a limo. He wanted to fool around with her, but she told him in no uncertain terms what to do to himself. She could not get the feeling of James' arms out of her head.

She had known for five years that he was somewhere in London. Well, she hadn't really known, but she had felt it in her bones. She hadn't tried to find him, but she knew he was out there somewhere.

She wasn't going to make a fool of herself, though, so at times she tried to block him out of her mind. Better not to go there, she thought. Maybe he's moved away, she told herself. Maybe he works for some big international company and he's been sent to the States. Wouldn't that be a laugh, her coming to his home town after all these years, and he whisks off to the States?

She never could get him completely off her mind, not even when she started to have other love affairs. It was never hard for her to find boyfriends, even if they were mostly all younger than her. She still had a good figure and an unlined face, and she wore the latest fashions, which made her look at least ten years younger than she was. These English rockers were fun guys, always a bit loony, the best of them, and she had a lot of wild times with them.

She never stopped thinking about James, though.

She wondered what he looked like now, what he was doing, where he lived, and if he ever thought about her or his son.

He stopped by her office the next day. She was bleary eyed and not in the best mood after her night out, and her ears were still ringing from the assault they'd suffered from the American's guitar.

He looked out of place in his pinstriped Navy blue suit and his button down shirt, standing in the cluttered, messy office that had plates of fish and chips and half-empty cups of tea scattered everywhere, with posters of rock stars in Day-Glo colors papering the walls, and sandalwood incense burning at a little Hindu shrine in a corner.

"Can I take you to lunch?" he said, standing over her desk. His eyes looked querulous, vulnerable.

Now is your chance, girl, a voice in her head said. You can let him have it with both barrels, after what he did to you.

She held her fire. Instead, she decided to make him squirm. "Sure," she said. "But I have expensive taste. You have to take me someplace nice. Like your club. I'm sure a man like you belongs to a stuffy old gentleman's club, right? Take me there."

"Women are only allowed at certain times," he said. "Not ordinarily for luncheon."

"Take me there," she said. "Or I'm not going out with you."

"I'm so sorry, but I can't do that."

Her head was pounding, her stomach was queasy, and all her jumpiness at seeing him again was displaced by the massive hangover she had. Now, she was just too angry to care.

"What's the matter, are you afraid your wife will find out?" she said. "Maybe she'll ask too many questions and upset the nice, settled life you have? I'm sure it must be lovely, living in some quiet, leafy suburb and taking the train into London every day, meeting your pals for lunch at your prim and proper club, while your wife stays home and plays bridge with her friends. Or do you still have a few children at home? A few little ones who came along after you left me? A few step-siblings to the son you have back in Philadelphia?

She felt the tears coming, but she bit her lip and held them back. She was not going to cry in front of him. She got up to go to the loo, just to get control of herself, but he grabbed her wrist.

"A son?" he said. "I didn't know what happened after you walked away from me. I didn't know if there was a baby at all, let alone if it was a boy or girl."

"It's a boy," Rosie said. "And he's 21 years old. You have a son who's a grown man, James."

He looked stricken. "I didn't know. I'm so sorry." Then, he straightened his shoulders. "Okay. I'll take you to my club. I'll probably get in trouble for this, but let's go."

And that's how it started. He took her to his ancient club, with its leather chairs and carpeted hallways and mahogany and brass furniture, and the waiters in their stiff uniforms raised their eyebrows and condescended to her, but she enjoyed every minute. She ordered soup and slurped it loudly, drank three glasses of champagne, and called every man she saw, "Mate".

Her headache went away but she didn't make things any easier for James. She brought up Pete every chance she could, telling him how beautiful and strong he was, what a perfect child.

Then she broke down when she told him that Pete was on his second tour of duty in Vietnam.

"I pray for him every night," she said, big tears dropping from her eyes onto the white linen tablecloth. "I've been away from him for so long, and I'm afraid something will happen to him now and I'll never forgive myself."

He gave her a clean napkin and she blew her nose loudly, then laughed bitterly. "I don't know why I'm telling you all this. It's not like you care. You wanted me to get rid of him in the first place."

His eyes looked pained. "Yes I did. I am sorry for that. I wasn't thinking clearly. I should have taken responsibility. It was despicable of me. Those were difficult times, though."

"Difficult?" she said. "That was nothing compared to raising a son by myself when I had so little money. I had to work two jobs sometimes just to put enough food on the table. My parents don't have much, so I couldn't count on them to help. One good thing about being over here is that I'm making better money than I would at home. London is the center of the world these days in the record industry, and I work right in the heart of the beast. I'm Harry Helms' right hand girl, I'm the big sister or mother for a whole stable of loony rockers, and Harry pays me well for it. I send money home every week, and my parents put it in a savings account for Pete. That way when he comes back from this war" -- she had to fight back tears again. "He'll have the money to get a start in life."

"I can help you out," James said. "I feel terrible that I walked away. Let me make it up to you. I can give you money for--"

"No!" she said, pounding her hand on the table. "No, no, no! I don't want your help. You weren't there when he was a baby, when he got sick with the measles and almost died, when he got beat up by the neighborhood bully, when he broke up with his first girlfriend. You weren't there for anything, and so I don't want your help now." She was shouting, she realized, and she turned to see all the tables around them had stopped their conversations and were staring at her.

"I understand," he said, speaking in a low tone. "I understand completely how you feel. Maybe there's something else I can do for him. I'm retired from the service, but I still know people in the Admiralty office, and they know people on the American side. I'm owed a few favors, and I could call them in. I could arrange to get him sent home. It would take going through some back channels, but I think I could do it."

Rosie felt like someone had punched her in the stomach. "You could do that? I don't believe you. Why would you do it? You've never met him. He's a stranger to you."

"Not entirely," James said. "He has some of you in him, and that makes me feel I know him, at least at second hand. I am sure he's got your fire, and your vivacity, and your intelligence, and your courage. I am sure he's a fine young man, and I want to help him."

Rosie wanted so much to tell him off, simply because she did not want anything from him now, nothing at all. But the promise of Pete's safety was too much to throw away. She had worried about him so much that she would be a fool to turn away from an offer of help.

"Okay," she said. "If you can help him, okay. Get him sent home as soon as possible. I keep worrying that his luck is going to run out, and I'll get a phone call from my mother some day telling me that she got a visit from a stone-faced Army officer telling her my son is not coming back." She bit her lip to keep from crying, and wiped her face with the napkin.

"I'll work on it right away," he said. "I have to warn you, though, that these things take time."

And then he asked to see her again. She was over him, so over him, but now she was indebted to him. She needed him to help Pete, and she couldn't just spit in his face and say goodbye when he held out the possibility of saving her son's life. And if it took time, then she had to put the time in.

So she said yes. And they went out. It was the strangest thing, because he did not seem to want to hide anything, even though he told her he was still married.

"Elizabeth and I have an understanding," he said. "We got married young, probably too young, and now the fire has gone out. We both know that, but we don't believe in divorce. So, we, well, we go our separate ways a lot now."

Rosie kept him at arm's length. "You can't walk back into my life after 20 years and act like everything is normal. It's not normal," she said. "It will never be normal."

And besides, she didn't know how he fit into her life. She was living in a crazy, upside down world where everything was changing, and there he was, still living in his button down 1950s world, looking as out of place in the sweaty little clubs she frequented as an accountant on a pirate ship.

He didn't like rock music, so that put him in the outer reaches of her universe. They settled into a routine where he took her out to lunch on Mondays, when she was recovering from her weekend excesses, and fed her a decent meal at his club with lots of water to flush the toxins out of her system. They spoke about his progress in getting Pete sent home, and she told him how things were going in her world -- how she was trying to sign that new band from Cornwall or Lancashire or keep last year's hot new band together while they squabbled about creative issues and acted like superstars on the strength of one measly regional hit record. He told her about the barrenness of his marriage, how he was only staying with Elizabeth so as to keep up appearances for the children, who were grown now but setting out on professional careers and not needing the distraction of a parental divorce.

In the good weather -- or, what passed for good weather in London -- they took walks down by the Thames and ate Swiss chocolate candies they bought at shops along the way. She often told him about her latest boyfriend, making it clear that he was nothing to her but a friend now -- and sometimes she cried on his shoulder about the caddish behavior of one more budding rock star who turned out to be less than a gentleman in spite of his angelic voice or sweet guitar playing.

And then came the day when he brought her a copy of an official letter from the Defense Department informing Corporal Pete Morley that he was being sent home immediately from Vietnam, and she was so excited she forgot herself and kissed him passionately. It was raining, and she knocked the umbrella out of his hand and stood there in the pouring rain on Marlborough street kissing him like she had never kissed a man before. Her heart was pounding, she was crying and laughing inside at the same time, and her legs were shaking. She didn't care that there were people passing by and staring at them, or that James was gripping her like a drowning man grabbing for a life raft. She could have made love to him right there, right on the street corner, she was so overcome.

They broke apart panting for breath, and she felt like her mouth was dry as the Sahara. He cleared his throat and looked away, but his face was flushed and his hands were shaking.

"Thank you," she said, trying to fill up the silence. "From the bottom of my heart. I don't know how you did that, but thank you."

"It was nothing," he said. "A small thing to do for my, ah, son." It was the first time he'd used that word. She felt a sudden urge to slap him, or kiss him again, she didn't know which. It was so crazy.

That was the first time she spent the night with him. He told her Elizabeth was visiting her sister in the country, and he was alone in the house. He invited her to stay, and she said no, but that he could come with her to the little flat she had in Soho. She took him there and they made love all night long on her little futon bed on the floor, stopping only to drink tea and look out the balcony window at the lights of London below them.

I don't know what I'm doing, she thought. I'm as mixed up as the musicians I deal with every day.

CHAPTER SIXTEEN

April 1968

Lucy was at St. Paul's Episcopal church in the basement conference room at 6:00 in the evening of April 4 stuffing envelopes with letters urging Congress to cut funding for the Vietnam War, and she had her little red transistor radio next to her on the table. She was listening to a Simon & Garfunkel tune when all of a sudden the song stopped: "We're breaking in to tell you that Dr. Martin Luther King Jr. has been shot, in Tennessee. Dr. King has been taken to the nearest hospital. Police are searching for the shooter. Stay tuned for more details as they come in."

It took her breath away, exactly like she had felt five years earlier when she heard President Kennedy had been shot.

She knew Dr. Denton was meeting with some students in his office upstairs. She suddenly felt she must tell him the news.

She rushed upstairs and down the carpeted hallway to the office at the end. The door was closed, and though she normally wouldn't disturb Dr. Denton when his door was closed, this was too important to wait. She knocked once and pushed the door open.

And what she saw made her step back in shock.

Later, recalling it, she remembered only a jumble of images, like a jigsaw puzzle that's been thrown on the ground, the pieces scattered everywhere.

There was Dr. Denton, bent over at the side of his desk, a white belly showing, face red and blotchy, eyes wide, hair askew, next to him a pair of tan legs splayed across the desk, bare feet with red toenails, jeans crumpled on the floor next to his feet, long hair in disarray, a face in the throes of emotion, eyes glaring at her in shock and disbelief.

"What are you doing here?" Dr. Denton shouted, his voice reverberating off the bookshelves, the pictures on the wall of him and various dignitaries, the awards, the diplomas. "Didn't you see the door was closed?"

"I, uh, wanted to tell you something," Lucy said. She could hardly get her mouth to move, and she stood there, frozen to the floor.

"Oh, my God," the girl said. She scrambled off the desk, hiding on the floor behind it.

The preacher managed to pull his pants up, tuck his shirt in, and straighten his hair in seconds. "For God's sake, what could possibly be that important?" he said. He was still breathing heavily, and his face was blazing.

"I just heard on the news, Dr. King was shot." She waited for the words to sink in. "I thought you should know right away."

His face registered shock. "Dr. King? When? Where?"

"I don't know all the details," she said. "It was in Tennessee, I think they said. It just happened. They're looking for the shooter."

"Is he dead?" There was sadness in the preacher's eyes.

"They said he was taken to the hospital. I guess we can only pray."

"Yes," Dr. Denton said. "We must pray. Let us all hold hands and pray for Dr. King's recovery." He held out one hand to Lucy, and the other to the disheveled, pretty blonde girl who was now standing beside him. She had somehow reached under the desk and grabbed her jeans, and managed to put them on while she was still hidden. She had on a tight, long-sleeved, tie-dyed blouse in blue and green, a leather wristlet, a peace pendant, and long blonde hair that was in serious need of brushing. She took Dr. Denton's hand without making eye contact with him or Lucy.

"Come, let us pray now," Dr. Denton said, waggling his fingers at Lucy. "He needs our prayers more than ever at this difficult time."

"No," Lucy said. "I will pray for him on my own." She turned and went out, closing the door behind her.

She went downstairs and closed the door to the conference room, taking her radio, which was blaring another news bulletin about Dr. King, and then left and took a bus home. She looked at the faces sitting around her and saw shock, disbelief, sadness, and anger on the faces of the black people, and some of the whites. Other whites chatted and laughed with each other as if nothing had happened, as if the world were still the same place it always was.

But it wasn't. It wasn't at all. It had changed so much. She knew that now. There was injustice and hatred and anger all around her, falsity and deceit, and conspiracy and shame and lies. Once again she saw, just as she had in the 1940s when Paul had betrayed her, that the world was a much grubbier, dirtier, sadder place than she had let herself believe. It was a place that snuffed out hope, pinched out the flame of goodness, a place that loved darkness more than light.

What a fool I've been, she thought. What a stupid fool. All around her she saw blindness and hate and destruction, and she realized her life these last years had been nothing but an illusion, nothing but false hope. Things weren't changing for the better, they were getting worse. There was no good in the world, only people all trying to get what they wanted, and pushing others out of the way to get it.

She got off the bus and walked the block home. The sun was going down and bathing everything in a dark red glow. She saw her neighbors sitting on their porches, heard staticky radios proclaiming that Dr. King was now dead, and saw a man washing his car at the curb while children played hopscotch nearby.

When she got to her house, Paul was sitting on the porch waiting for her.

"I heard the news," he said. "It's terrible, isn't it?"

Lucy walked up the steps and sat down next to him on the little porch swing. He had gotten so thin in the last year, and his white hair stood up on top of his head like the fibers of a wire brush. His blue eyes seemed to burn from his face, and his skin was almost translucent, an old man's skin. His hands trembled in his lap and his head was twitching just slightly, but he looked at her with such peace in his eyes that it took her breath away.

She sat down next to him and just looked at him for a few moments. He smiled, and she was overcome by the feeling of his love for her. Through all the turmoil of their lives together, all the seismic shocks, he had stayed. He had made many mistakes, and he had paid the price for them, but she knew his love for her had never wavered.

She looked out at the world around her, realizing what a fool she'd been. She'd spent the last eight years chasing a dream, an illusion, an infatuation, seduced by the golden voice and good looks and high-flying words of a man who had turned out to be no better than any other person on this Earth.

Paul put his hand on hers and squeezed it. She saw, as if for the first time, how much of a toll his disease had taken on him these last few years. While she had been off on her crusade he'd lost ground. He was a sick old man now, holding on to life with both hands, but he hadn't complained, hadn't asked for any sympathy.

"Does Dr. Denton know about the shooting?" he said. "Has he heard the news?"

"Yes," she said. "I told him. I caught him with. . . one of the college girls. In his office. It was disgusting."

Paul didn't seem surprised. "Oh, I figured that was going on. I saw the way some of those girls looked at him. And the way he sort of put his shoulders back and preened around them."

"You did?" Lucy said. "How did you see that? I never noticed it. I thought he was too high-minded to do anything like that."

"Oh, we're all fallen creatures," Paul said. "We're capable of good and bad. And someone in his position, well, you start to think you can do no wrong."

He shook his head ruefully, perhaps remembering what that felt like in his own life.

"I feel like such a fool," Lucy said. "I took so much time away from you, from us. I gave so much of my precious time to that man. I wish I had it back."

"No!" Paul said, his querulous voice suddenly loud. "Every minute you spent was for a good cause. What you did mattered in people's lives, even if you got fooled by a handsome face and a musical voice. Things need to change, Lucy. There's so much injustice, and you did your part to correct that. You made a difference, and I'm proud of you."

"Thank you," Lucy said. "I don't know how much difference I made, but it's nice to hear you say that."

"Now, I have something to show you," Paul said. He reached a shaking hand in his pants pocket, and pulled out a piece of paper. He unfolded it carefully, and tried to get his hand to stop trembling long enough to read it. It said "Western Union" on the top of it, and Lucy's heart jumped in her chest. A telegram could only mean bad news about either Rosie, or Pete, who was in a hospital somewhere in Southeast Asia.

"What is it?" she shouted. "Please don't tell me something bad has happened. Is it Rosie? Is it Pete? I knew he shouldn't have enlisted. I knew it."

Paul put his hand on her shoulder. "Don't worry, dear. It's not anything bad. It's from the Army. You remember Pete was wounded in a battle over there, and he's in the hospital. He's recovered from the wound, and he's being sent home. He's coming home, Lucy!"

There were tears in his eyes. She saw how much he loved the boy, and what a strain it had been, worrying about him while he was

116

away at war. She had thought she was the only one losing sleep over Pete, worrying about every phone call that came, wondering when the doorbell rang if it was bad news about the boy. The strain had been unbearable, especially when Pete re-enlisted and did a second tour of duty, just as the fighting escalated.

She reached over and put her arms around her husband, feeling his thin, trembling shoulders through his clothes. He was trying to get control of himself, but the trembling only worsened, and she had to hold him a long time and soothe him with her voice before his body finally stopped shaking. She stroked his hair and whispered in his ears, and finally he took a deep breath and seemed to relax.

It was 7:00 in the evening, and although the sun had gone down the sky was still bathed in its afterglow. Lights were going on in houses up and down the street, and the children had gone in for their supper. The only person still out was old Paddy Boyle, the Irishman who lived across the street. Lucy could see him smoking his pipe and sitting in his rocking chair reading the Evening Bulletin newspaper, the way he always did. His daughter had gone over to Ireland five years ago after Paddy's wife died and brought him back to Philadelphia, and although he was a pleasant enough man, he didn't like his new home. He talked of Ireland all the time, and seemed disturbed at all the "mad hubbub" of America.

"Are you better now?" Lucy said, stroking Paul's hair.

"Yes," he said. "You know, I don't sleep very well anymore. I'm always in a half-sleep, and I wake up a lot. I get these dreams. . . hear my mother's voice. Last night I saw the old man, my father, for the first time in years. He was standing there big as life, smiling at me. Grinning like he used to, and then he launched into one of his

117

old Irish songs. I haven't thought about him in so long. I wonder if the old scoundrel is in Heaven? Do you think God would have him?"

Lucy smiled. "I think there's mercy for all of us," she said.

"Good," Paul said. "That makes me feel better. Maybe there's a place for me too."

"I'm going to go inside now and fix us some dinner," Lucy said. "Why don't you come in and find out what the latest news is about the assassination?"

"In a minute," Paul said. "I see Paddy Boyle over there on his porch. I think I'll go over and say hello to him. The poor old soul misses his home in Ireland. He doesn't fit in over here, and he knows it. I'll go pass the time with him for a few minutes. You know, he comes from Cork, which is down the road from Skibbereen, and he likes to talk about horse racing over there, at the Cork racetrack. He's mad about the ponies."

"Okay," Lucy said. "You do that. It will do Paddy good to talk for awhile. I'll call you when dinner's ready."

Lucy went inside and stood at the sink washing her hands, thinking about what to make for dinner. She was drying her hands off with a towel when she heard yelling outside in the street. She rushed out and saw Paul lying on the sidewalk in front of their porch. Next to him was Paddy Boyle, who was shouting at the top of his lungs for someone to help.

"What's the matter?" Lucy said, coming down the steps. "What happened?"

"Why, it was the strangest thing," Paddy said. "I was sittin' on the porch, mindin' me business, when your man there called to me that he was comin' over to say hello, and as I watched he tumbled headfirst down the steps onto the pavement. Oh, he hit it with a terrible crash, missus. You see, there's blood comin' out of his ear there. He wasn't steady on his feet, I think. Had he been drinkin' do you suppose?"

"Paul!" Lucy cried, cradling his head in her arms. "Paul, what happened?"

He did not answer.

And then she realized that for the first time in a long time he was still, his body had stopped trembling. There was a quiet about him that was different. "Paul," she said, through tears. "Please answer me, Paul."

"God rest his soul," Paddy said, blessing himself. "I think he's gone, missus. I saw a man tumble off a horse once at the racetrack, and he fell like that, on his head. It's not a thing you recover from. If you don't mind me sayin', I think you should call a priest."

CHAPTER SEVENTEEN

October 23, 1962

It was just a fragment of a dream, and she could not remember much when she woke up, just the image of Lorenzo pointing and smiling. She thought of him as she ate breakfast by herself in the elegant hotel restaurant, with the waiters in their white shirts and black pants, their black shoes polished to a mirror brightness. The newspaper headlines blared out the news that U.S. warships were headed to Cuba. There were people sitting in the TV room, but Mercy chose not to go in. She did not want to hear the latest news. She preferred to go about her business like everything was normal. It was the only way she could function.

At 9:00 sharp the doorman came in to the restaurant and told her that a cab was waiting outside for her. She went out to see Lorenzo holding the door to the cab for her, beaming as if he was on top of the world. He took off his baseball cap and bowed once again.

It was a brilliant late October day, not a cloud anywhere, blue squares of the sky showing through the tops of the tall buildings and the sun making everything look fresh and clean.

"To the Philadelphia Museum of Art, correct?" he said, when he got behind the wheel. "One of the world's finest art museums, you know."

It was the strangest thing, because he didn't look scared or grim, like everyone else. He was his same upbeat, cheery self. Did he not know the news?

But no, he had the radio turned to a news station, and she could hear the announcer's tense staccato voice reciting the latest news bulletin. Lorenzo turned the sound down as soon as he got in the car, but Mercy had heard it.

"So, what do you think about this crisis?" Mercy said.

"I think," he said, "that I am glad I have the day off, and I get to drive a beautiful woman like you around. If that crazy Krushchev is going to start peppering us with nuclear missiles, well, I couldn't think of a better way to spend my last hours on Earth."

Mercy blushed. "I think the stress has gone to your head, Lorenzo. There must be better things to do than drive me around if this is your last day on Earth."

"No," he said. "This is exactly how I want to spend my time. And, say, there's a bonus: I get to look at paintings in one of the greatest art museums on the planet."

"Actually," she said, "I'm not going to look at the paintings. I have a meeting with someone there. But I suppose you could look at some paintings while you're waiting for me."

"An excellent idea," he said. He weaved in and out of the downtown traffic, a smile on his face. "You must be an important person, having meetings with officials at the art museum."

"Oh, no," she said. "I'm just here to do some research about movies. Old movies. The silents."

"Is that so? I love those old movies myself. Charlie Chaplin, Buster Keaton, all of them. I'm a film buff. My Dad was involved in

121

the movie industry around here. Did you know at one time Philadelphia was a center of filmmaking?"

"I did," she said. "There was a man named Siegmund Lubin who had a studio."

"Pops Lubin? You know about him?" Lorenzo said, whistling. "Small world, isn't it? That's the studio my Dad worked at."

Mercy was thunderstruck. "Your father? What did he do? Was he an actor?"

"No, nothing like that," Lorenzo said, chuckling. "No, he was a carpenter. He helped to build the sets. It was when old man Lubin had his studio at 27th and Indiana streets. He needed a lot of workers to build things for him, and my Dad made himself useful. He was a new immigrant, could barely speak any English, but he was good with his hands. Lubin was an immigrant himself, so he had a soft spot for my father, I guess. He helped him out, gave him employment."

"Did you work there too?"

"Now, listen, Mercy, I know I have the appearance of a man of great antiquity, but I'm not that old!" Lorenzo said, chuckling. "I consider myself a young man, a mere stripling. No, I was just a kid when my Dad worked for Pops Lubin. That was before the First World War, you understand. It was only for a few years, when they made the films in the city here. Dad didn't move out there in the country when Lubin set up his big studio. No, he was only connected with the one in the city. He always said it was the most interesting time of his life, working for Pops. It was magical, he said, being involved in this whole business of making dreams come alive.

"I mean, think about it," he continued. "This was an amazing invention. Poor people like my parents came here from their little villages, and they'd never seen anything like that. They must have been goggle eyed, to look into those old nickelodeon machines and see people riding horses, shooting each other, kissing pretty girls -- why, it must have been like a miracle to them. And later, when they'd go into a movie house and see those stories on a screen, I bet they must have felt like it was magic."

"Well, it is, in a way," Mercy said. "But like all magic, it's an illusion. There are a lot of little men running around inside the machine, so to speak. The movie stars are all regular people, just like us. I've lived long enough in California to know that. People don't want to hear that, but it's true."

"Oh sure," Lorenzo said. "My Dad used to tell me what went on behind the scenes, how they filmed things, the way they used lighting and makeup to make the actresses look more beautiful than they were. But, he always said that wasn't worth thinking about. We all need a bit of the illusion, just to get through our days, he would tell me."

He turned up the hill leading to the monumental facade of the Museum Of Art, built to look like a Greek Temple on top of a hill overlooking the silver ribbon of the Schuykill River. He pulled the cab into the parking lot, turned the engine off, and raced around and opened the door for Mercy.

"Here we are," he said, sweeping his arm to encompass the Art Museum's huge fluted columns, the statues of gods and goddesses, and the grand staircase leading to the entrance. "Isn't it magnificent? I get goose bumps every time I come here."

"Yes," Mercy said. "I don't know how long I'll be. Should I just let you go and call a cab when I'm finished?"

"Certainly not," Lorenzo said. He reached inside and turned the meter off. "I told you, this is my day off. I informed the dispatcher that I have a special client I'm working for all day. I'm yours as long as you need me, and you don't have to pay while I'm waiting."

"That's very nice of you," Mercy said. "But I hate to make you wait for me."

"Not at all," Lorenzo said. "I'm off the clock, as I already mentioned. And I'll be making myself busy, don't you worry. I love this place, and I intend to spend my time looking at the paintings. I have quite a few favorites in there, and I'm going to look them up. They're like old friends to me."

Mercy had spoken on the phone to the contact Nelson had given her: a man named Henry Mortenson, who was head of the Asian Art section of the museum. "He's a friend and business contact," Nelson had said, "but more important, he's an aficionado of silent films. He's from Old Money in Philadelphia -- his father owned a construction company that built commercial buildings, and they're filthy rich. He collects artifacts of the silent film era, and he knows about Lubin and his company."

Mercy headed for the side door of the museum, where Mortenson had told her to enter, and Lorenzo followed along.

"I've never been in this part of the museum," Lorenzo said. "I guess this is the employees' entrance?"

"Yes, that's what I've been told."

They were met at the door by a security guard in a gray uniform. "May I help you?" he said.

"I'm here to see Henry Mortenson," Mercy said. "Certainly," the guard said. "To get to his office you go down the hallway and make a left, then it's the third door on the right. I can show you the way. Are you with her, sir?" he said to Lorenzo. It was obvious he thought Lorenzo was some kind of workman who had gone in the wrong door.

"I'm her knight in shining armor," Lorenzo said. "Although she doesn't need me at the present, I am ready to defend her against dragons, ogres, and monsters of every stripe. I will be upstairs, roaming around among the Impressionist paintings, but should my lady need me, she can just whistle and I'll be there." He gave a grand bow, then headed off in the direction of an elevator.

"Interesting man," the guard said, when he left. "Yes," Mercy said, watching the way Lorenzo strutted along like a knight errant, if they could be imagined to strut. "He's a unique man."

The guard led Mercy down a long tiled hallway that echoed with the sound of radio news reports from every office about the missile crisis. At the end of the hallway they made a left, then the guard opened a wooden door and there was a large desk with a young blonde secretary sitting behind it, clacking away on a typewriter. She had a little black transistor radio on her desk, but the volume was turned down low and Mercy couldn't make out what the announcer was saying.

The secretary stood up and said, "Miss Francis? Nice to you meet you. Mr. Mortenson is waiting for you. This way, please." She opened the door to an inner office where Henry Mortenson was sitting behind his teak desk with Japanese prints on the wall behind him. He rose and gave Mercy a hearty handshake, and looked happy to see her. He had a patrician, WASPy face with sandy blonde hair brushed to one side, a Navy blue pinstriped suit with a red carnation in the lapel, and steel gray eyes behind his horn-rimmed glasses.

He motioned for her to sit down across from him, and he sat on the edge of his desk and smiled grimly.

"Well, you've certainly come at an interesting time," he said. "I don't know if you heard the radios on your way down the hall, but every office has a radio blaring out the latest bulletins about this damned missile crisis. I refuse to tune in, myself. I am not going to get caught up in this."

"It's upsetting," Mercy said. "To think that we could be in a nuclear war. The news seems to be getting worse by the minute."

"Damned fool politicians," Mortenson said. "Them and the generals. It's criminal, the way they keep getting us into these situations. They ought to be shot."

He went around to his big leather chair and sat down. "I have to say, though, that the one thing my job has taught me is to take a longer view of things. Why, we have Chinese paintings in our collection that were done more than 1500 years ago. You know what some of them are about? Battles. War has unfortunately been part of man's existence for millennia. It always has been, and always will be. Somehow, we have survived. That's what I think of at a time like this. That humanity will somehow survive."

"I hope you're right," Mercy said.

"Enough of this gloom and doom talk," Mortenson said, slapping his palm on the table for emphasis. "How is Nelson? I haven't seen the old matinee idol in ages. How is he doing?"

"Oh, fine," Mercy said. Nelson had told her to keep his condition a secret, so she tried to appear cheerful.

"Henry Mortenson is a fine old blueblood," Nelson had said, "but sometimes they're the ones you have to watch the most. I don't want any vultures circling me, smelling blood, expecting to get bargains on my paintings because I'm on my way out."

"Nelson is the same as ever," she said to Mortenson. "Ornery at times, when he's not worshipping at the altar of his greatness."

"Well, he's entitled," Mortenson said. "He was quite an actor at one time. I've seen his films. The man had talent. It's a shame what happened to him, but he wasn't the only silent film star to retire early because of, ah, indiscretions. But we all have skeletons in our closet, don't we?" he said, shrugging his shoulders. "I'm sure every person in public life has something they'd rather the world didn't know about."

"We muddle through the best we can," Mercy said. "We have proud moments and embarrassing ones."

Just then Mortenson's blonde secretary poked her head in the door. "Can I get anyone coffee?"

"Yes, thank you," Mercy said.

"I'll have a cup," Mortenson said. "Thank you, Louise."

127

The secretary closed the door, but she was back almost immediately, carrying a tray with cups and saucers, a coffee pot, plus sugar and cream.

She set it down on the edge of Mortenson's desk, then left.

Mortenson poured a cup of coffee for Mercy, then one for himself. As he and Mercy stirred their cream and sugar into their cups, he said, "Well, let's get down to business. Nelson said you're here to research the old Lubin factory, right?"

"Not exactly," Mercy said. "Oh, I'd like to see what's left of the factory, but I'm really more interested in any prints of his films. Nelson is trying to add to his collection of silent films."

"I know he is, the old dog," Mortenson said, sipping from his cup. "I've been on the trail of some of those things myself, and I know he's sniffing around too. The problem is that so many of them are gone, you know. They were destroyed in fires, or lost, or the chemicals in them oxidized, and they're useless.

"You know, it's funny that I have an interest in these old films," he continued. "My specialty is Asian art, and the great master painters from that tradition were skilled at creating timeless scenes, landscapes that seem almost eternal, outside of time. Waterfalls, mountains in the distance, a crane in flight, mist. There is a sense of great serenity that comes from looking at them. It's so different than the ephemeral nature of film. So many old films have been lost, and they weren't really made with the future in mind anyway."

"It was a new medium," Mercy said. "And from what I know, they were all making it up as they went along. They basically made up an art form in a decade or two."

"Oh, yes," he said. "And they weren't all the type of men you'd invite to dinner, you know. Pops Lubin was known for stealing other people's ideas. He had the soul of a pirate. He wasn't thinking about art, he was thinking of the cash register. They all were. The amazing thing is, they created art anyway." He looked out the window, at the city skyline, dominated by the City Hall tower and its statue of William Penn looking out at the city he founded. "It's funny how beautiful things develop from the simplest impulses. The people who came to this country in the beginning, they were a mix of good and bad, noble souls and scoundrels. Why, the folks who founded some of our greatest institutions made their fortunes in the slave trade, or had blood on their hands in other ways. And yet here we are, preserving the treasures of Western art, making sure that the beautiful things in this world aren't lost."

"It's important work," Mercy said, "preserving beauty. And those old movies were amazing, weren't they? The actors had to be so expressive because they had no sound or color to work with. The directors used light and shadows, subtlety in the words, and dramatic gestures to communicate so much emotion."

Mortenson put his cup down and looked at her. "I can see you're not just Nelson's secretary, are you? You have a real feel for this art form."

"Oh, I didn't even know much about it till Nelson got me started on this project," she said, scoffing. "I know art, but I didn't care much about film -- then he started showing me some of his old two reelers, and I was enthralled."

"Did he tell you that he worked for Lubin?" Mortenson said.

"Yes," Mercy said. "In fact, that's the big reason why he wants me to find some prints. He's trying to locate every film he ever appeared in."

"I should have known!" Mortenson said, laughing. "Of course Nelson would have a personal interest in this. He's building a shrine to himself out there in California! The man has an ego as big as Los Angeles."

"Yes, he's his own biggest fan," Mercy said. "But, he's been a good friend to me, and I want to help him out."

"Well, in that case I'll put you on the right track," Mortenson said. "I happen to know there's a man in Montgomery County who has some of the old two reelers stored in his garage. He was a farmer and a sort of handyman who lived next to Lubin's Betzwood studio for many years. You know Lubin lost his European market during the First World War and he went bankrupt in 1917? He abandoned his Betzwood studio after that, and the place was deserted. Apparently this man came into a lot of material from the studio. Don't ask me how," he said, arching his eyebrows ironically.

"Can I meet him?" Mercy said. "I'd like to talk to him."

"Of course. His name's Jonah Martin. He's an old codger now, though, and he's not the most sociable fellow. I can give you his phone number, and you can see if you can talk him into meeting with you."

"Do you know his address?" Mercy said. "I'd like to drive there today and try to meet him."

Mortenson raised his eyebrows. "Today? That's kind of quick, isn't it?"

Mercy jerked her thumb at the sound of the radio coming from the secretary's desk outside the door. "I think under the circumstances time is at a premium, don't you? I just would like to do whatever I can right now, rather than waiting. Plus, it keeps me from going crazy, if you know what I mean."

Mortenson smiled wryly. "I understand." He pulled out a pen and scribbled something on a notepad on his desk, then ripped the sheet off, folded it, and handed it to Mercy. "Here it is. I met Jonah Martin once, so I can tell you he's a crotchety old boy. I wish you luck with him. Just warning you that he may slam the door in your face. However, under the circumstances I don't blame you for going out there."

"Thank you," Mercy said. She stood up and held out her hand. "You've been a big help. It was nice to meet you. I hope we meet again."

Mortenson laughed. "I do too, Mercy. I do too."

CHAPTER EIGHTEEN

April 10, 1968

The funeral was on a typical early Spring day in Philadelphia, where the sun is shining brightly, but as soon as you step into the shadows an icy chill goes through you. The old stone St. Malachy's church was cold and drafty, and Lucy sat in the first pew with Rosie next to her. She had called overseas to Rosie to tell her the news, and Rosie booked the first available flight to come home. She arrived looking like a gypsy, with a multicolored bandana on her head, a feather boa, long paisley coat and a striped miniskirt and white boots.

She was distraught about Paul's death, sobbing on Lucy's shoulder as soon as she got out of the cab from the airport. "I should have been here," she sobbed. "I ran away, I never should have left, I'm so sorry."

Lucy patted her hair and said, "Don't do that, Rosie. You did what you had to do. He didn't suffer. He just fell down the steps, hit his head and died. It could have been worse."

Rosie spent the night before the funeral looking at old pictures with Lucy, and talking about her life in London, how exciting it was to be there, the many eccentric characters she had met, the adventures she'd had. Lucy could tell she was not in any hurry to come back home, even though she kept saying, "I'll be here for you, Mom. You can count on me."

Lucy had tried to reach Rosie's son Pete, calling a phone number she had from the last official letter she'd received about Pete's discharge from the Army, but she couldn't locate him. He had been released from the hospital, but nobody in Washington seemed to know where he was, and when she made a long distance call to the hospital in Thailand that he had been in, the line was full of static and it went dead after a few seconds. She wanted to delay Paul's funeral for an extra few days, but Rosie told her she had to get back to London.

"We're in the middle of negotiations to sign a band that could be huge," she said. "Harry needs me back there to help out."

So, Lucy had given in and scheduled the funeral for this chilly day, and she sat numbly through the service, listening to the priest talk in the cone-shaped halo from the stained glass window behind him about how we all live in the hope of resurrection, and how we must live as if every day our life could end and we could be standing before God accounting for our time here.

She hoped that God would take into account the good that Paul did, and weigh it against his failings and imperfections. The arc of his life had been tragic in some ways -- a father who abandoned him, the corruption of material success, the seduction by the hateful message of the Nazis, a prison term, and breaking his marital vows too. But in all the debris of his life there had been some shining moments like diamonds glinting in a rubbish pile. He had spent the long years of his penance never complaining, never feeling sorry for himself, always being there as a strong, silent presence in the lives of people around him. He had been a wise, strong figure in the life of his grandson Pete, guiding him with a word here or there, always gentle, never harsh, no matter how many mistakes Pete made in his tortured journey toward adulthood. He had worked with Lucy to do what they could to better the lives of black people, and he had been a voice that stood against injustice wherever he saw it. Always with kindness, though, never anger. The anger had gone out of him a long, long time ago.

Lucy was surprised to see the number of people who turned up for the funeral. There were some familiar faces from the Civil Rights and Peace movements, and one or two old friends, but there were other people she did not recognize. Afterward, outside the church, people came up to her and introduced themselves. They were ordinary people that Paul had been kind to over the years, like Joe Goldstein, who owned the lunch counter on 23rd street, who said Paul came in many days for lunch and always had a kind word for his retarded son who worked behind the counter. Or, old Mrs. Bunting, who walked with a cane, and who said Paul used to do her grocery shopping for her, bringing the bags in her house and putting everything away. Or, Ralph Bunscome, the black bus driver who said Paul used to sit and drink coffee with him in the bus terminal and who said Paul was a great comfort to him after his wife died.

She realized then that Paul had made a difference in these people's lives, and it was a side of him that she had not known about.

She looked in vain for Pete, still hoping even at the cemetery that he would turn up, but he never did. She knew he would have been there if he could, or at least she thought that way.

"Maybe he's staying away on purpose," Rosie said. "Maybe he doesn't want to see me."

"Oh, I can't believe that," Lucy said. "You're his mother."

"He hasn't written to me in a year," Rosie said. "I worry about him all the time, write him letters all the time, but he never answers. I think he hates me. I've been a horrible mother."

She stayed up all night after the funeral weeping, and Lucy had to comfort her. She tried to tell Rosie she had been a good mother, not to worry, that Pete would come around, but Rosie swore her life had been a failure, she was going to burn in Hell for abandoning her parents and her son, and that she was an evil person. She promised Lucy she would come back and take care of her, that she would make up for all her past mistakes.

By the morning she had cried herself out, and she took a shower and changed into an outfit that made her look like a combination Afghan princess and tent show queen, and she teetered along on six inch heels.

"My cab will be here shortly," she said. "I have to get back, Mom, you understand, right? I'll wrap things up as fast as I can, but I'll be back in a matter of months for good. Well, it might take a little longer. Six months, a year -- I don't know. But I promise I'm coming back. You take care of yourself. And tell Pete I love him, and I'm coming back soon."

And then she was gone, down the steps and out to the waiting yellow cab, which sped off with a roar of its engine.

CHAPTER NINETEEN

July 1968

"Is Betty Taylor there?"

The woman behind the screen door was large and had skin the color of eggplant, and she looked at Pete with mistrust in her eyes. She had on a blue dress with white polka dots and a white apron covering it, and she was wiping her hands with a dish towel. From within the neat row home there came the smell of ham and sweet potatoes. Pete could hear a radio in the room behind her, and the sound of a gospel preacher's rhythmic chanting voice.

"What do you want with Betty?" the woman said.

"I, uh, have something for her," Pete said. He was conscious of a group of black children behind him on the street, whispering and staring at him. "It's something from Luther." At the mention of Luther's name the woman's eyes widened, but she still made no motion to let him in.

"I was in 'Nam with him," Pete said. "I was there when he died."

The woman seemed to soften. "You were?" she said. "You the boy who took the letter to Luther's parents?"

Pete nodded. "That was me."

"Brave of you, coming down here so soon after Dr. King's death. Or maybe foolish, I don't know."

"I thought it was important," Pete said.

"Wait here." She turned from the door and went back inside, and Pete could hear voices, a discussion going on. "You sit out there, don't go no further," he heard the black woman say. "On the porch. If anything happen, you call me."

Pete turned and waved at the black children, who scattered like a flock of birds after a stone is thrown at it.

A slim black girl in a yellow flowered dress, buttoned up to her neck, came to the door and opened it part way. She had skin the color of coffee with cream, and her eyes were dark and almond shaped. Her features seemed a combination of Middle Eastern and African, and she was beautiful.

"I'm Betty Taylor," she said. "Who are you?"

"My name is Pete Morley," he said. "I met your, ah, friend Luther in Viet Nam. I was there when he died. I have something to give you."

Her lip quivered, but she mastered herself. "What is it?"

"Can we sit down?" Pete said, pointing to the porch swing. "My leg is hurting me." He was still walking with a cane because his leg hadn't completely healed from the shrapnel he took at Hue, and it was throbbing.

"Okay." She came outside and sat down on the swing. Pete eased himself down next to her. She folded her hands in her lap and waited. The children in the street had gradually come back, and they were standing on the sidewalk watching them.

She didn't waste any time. "Where is it?" she said. "This thing from Luther."

He reached in his pocket and pulled out the lighter. "Here," he said, handing it to her.

She took the small silver square and turned it over. There was an engraving on it that said, "To Sweetness, from Peaches. Love forever."

She smiled. "I gave that to him last year. He smoked too much, but I couldn't get him to stop. I thought at least this way he'd think of me every time he lit up."

"Everybody smoked over there," Pete said. "Although it wasn't easy, because it rained so much. That lighter came in handy, though, in the rain."

It was a Sunday in early July, and the air was still. The street was quiet, except for the children, who had gotten bored with watching Pete and went back to their games, hopscotch for the girls, and a form of basketball for the boys that involved shooting a tennis ball through a rickety hoop nailed to a telephone pole.

"Did you know him well over there?" Betty said. "What was he like in Viet Nam?"

Pete cleared his throat. She seemed to want him to say something. Her wide brown eyes searched his face. "I, uh, well, he was a brave soldier," he said.

"You don't have to lie," she said. "I can see you didn't know him very well. He wasn't no brave soldier, I know that. Luther Copeland was scared every minute he was there, I'm sure. He was only there because he got drafted."

"Everybody was scared over there," Pete said. "No exceptions."

"Makes no difference to me," Betty said. "I don't care that he was afraid of getting his head shot off halfway around the world. That doesn't matter at all. He was brave in other ways. He was a good, churchgoing man. He treated people right. You know, when they had the riots on Columbia Avenue in '64 he was only 12 years old, and he stood in front of Bernstein's Appliance store and hollered at the people trying to loot the place. He told them they ought to be ashamed, stealing TVs from that man's store. His Mama had to come get him before the people beat him up."

"He sounds like a special man," Pete said. "I wish I had known him better."

She stared at him for what seemed like a full minute, appraising him. Finally, she looked away, and said, "It's been a month since his funeral. I cry myself to sleep every night, but you know what scares me? I'm having a hard time remembering his face. We only started dating the last year of high school, and I don't have that many pictures of him. My Mama told me when somebody close to you dies you go through a time when you think the memory is fading, but it comes back eventually. I'm scared it won't come back."

"Oh, I'm sure it will," Pete said. "My mother's been in England for six years, and that happened to me when she first went away. I can see her in my mind now, though."

Betty sighed and looked at her hands folded in her lap. "Tell me what you knew about him, please," she said.

Pete shifted uncomfortably in the swing. He didn't know what to do. He hardly knew Luther, and this girl was too smart to lie to.

"I, uh, I only met him for a short time," Pete said. "We were holed up in a house during the fighting in Hue. It was a crazy morning, with a lot of action. His unit got destroyed by mortar fire, and he was just trying to take cover. He was grateful to be out of the fire, I think. So was I. We talked for a bit. He told me about you."

"He did?" Betty said. "What did he say?"

"He said you were the best thing that ever happened to him," Pete said. "And that's the truth."

"How did he die?" she said.

"I didn't really see it," Pete said. "A sergeant came along and ordered us to get to a house up the street where some of our men were holed up. We started out, dodging bullets all the way, and Luther got hit. He was behind me, so I didn't see it happen."

She tightened her hands into fists, and her face got hard. "Why did you do it?"

"Do what?"

"Why did you go back and get the lighter? What made you do that, and bring it here to me?"

Pete shook his head. "I don't know. He seemed like a nice kid. I, uh, I never really talked to a black man that much. It just seemed so unfair that he got killed. I thought it was the right thing to do. I could have been friends with him, I think."

She looked at him, and her dark eyes narrowed. "You do? I wonder. Would you have worked next to him? He was ready to go to trade school before he got his draft notice. He wanted to be an electrician. Would you do business with him, Mr. Morley? Would you have hired him to do a job for you?"

"Sure," Pete said. "If he was smart enough to learn that trade, I'd have used him."

"Smart enough?" she said. "Oh, so you don't think people down here can learn all about electronics, right? That's what kept us out of the trade unions all these years. Folks like you thinking we're not smart enough."

"You're putting words in my mouth," Pete said. "I didn't say he wasn't smart. Hell, I'm probably not smart enough to be an electrician."

There was an uncomfortable silence, and Pete wondered why he had taken the time to come here. He wasn't having any luck delivering these letters. He'd already gone to Luther's parents' house two days ago, and Luther's mother had simply grabbed the letter from his hand and slammed the door in his face.

The letter. He had almost forgotten the letter. He reached in his pocket and pulled it out. Betty saw the handwriting on the envelope and her eyes got bigger. "Is that from Luther?" she said.

"Yes," he said, handing it over. "It's for you."

She tore it open with trembling hands, and began reading silently. It was two pages, in a neat, precise handwriting with nothing crossed out. She put her hand to her mouth, so Pete could not see, but he thought she was struggling to keep from crying out. She gasped once or twice, and blinked away tears.

Finally, when she had gotten to the end of the letter, she folded the pages neatly and put them back in the envelope. She took a deep breath and looked away for a moment, then said, "Thank you, Mr. Morley, for bringing this to me. And the lighter, too. I appreciate it. Now, if you don't mind, I think it's time you should go." She stood up and held out her hand for him to shake.

He stood up and took her hand. His leg tightened up and he winced with pain.

"Are you all right?" she said, suddenly full of concern.

"It's okay," he said. "The muscles tighten up when I sit for too long."

"Is that a battle wound?" she said.

"Yes. The same battle Luther was killed in. I got hit by shrapnel. Had to spend six weeks in the hospital. I wanted to go back, but they sent me home, said I was done. I don't know how it happened, though, because I saw guys get sent back with worse injuries than what I have."

"Maybe you have someone watching out for you," Betty said. "Luther didn't have that advantage. He was just an ordinary black man, sent over to someplace he never heard of, and told to kill people in a war that didn't make sense to him."

"He was an American," Pete said. "We're fighting communism over there, and he was doing his duty. It was the patriotic thing to do."

She looked at him like he was a child. "You really believe that?" she said.

"Sure I do. There's right and there's wrong. We're on the side of right."

She shook her head, and seemed to make up her mind. "Goodbye Mr. Morley," she said. "Have a nice day." She turned on her heel and went through the front door, letting the screen door slam behind her.

Pete limped down the three steps to the porch and then started on his way to the subway. He felt the eyes of the black kids staring at him, and it reminded him of the way the Vietnamese children stared when he went into their villages. Like he was an alien, a creature from another reality, and they didn't know what to expect from him. He felt their eyes burning into his back as he passed, and he knew he wasn't welcome. The street was neat and well-kept, a lot like the street he lived on with his grandparents in West Philly, although there were some posters on the telephone poles advertising speeches by Black Muslim leaders, and he heard a radio playing with what sounded like a fiery black power speaker. "Tell me, what has America ever done for the Black man?" the voice roared.

As Pete moved down the street slowly, he wondered what it had done for him. He had been a supporter of George Wallace for president, even gone to some rallies for him, had thought the country was going to hell, with all the hippies and the anti-war crazies and the blacks stirring up trouble. "We have to get back to what made this country great," he would tell people. "That's all we need. It's simple."

Now he wished it were that simple.

CHAPTER TWENTY

October 23, 1962

Mortenson walked Mercy out of his office and down the hallway, where she said, "Can I get to the Impressionist section of the museum from here?"

"Sure," Mortenson said. "Take that elevator over there to the third floor, then turn right and you'll be there.

Mercy said goodbye to him and took the elevator up to the third floor, then went down a long hallway to the Impressionist section. She found Lorenzo studying a large painting by Auguste Renoir, of some rosy-cheeked women sitting at a table in a sunlit cafe.

He was standing about twenty feet away from the painting with his arms folded across his chest, a look of beatific joy on his face.

"Isn't it beautiful?" he said, when she approached him. "I think there was no painter in history like Renoir. A master, beyond a doubt. Look at the way he uses light! I think he must have known more about light than any human ever. Doesn't it just lift you up, the way light radiates out from the faces of those girls? How can you do that with just a few dabs of oil on canvas? It's a magnificent thing."

"Yes, it's amazing, what he does," Mercy said.

"How can people even think of destroying that?" Lorenzo said. "Of destroying all the beautiful works of art, the music, the sculpture, the literature. It's a crime, ma'am, it really is. I hope our leaders come to their senses."

"I do too, Lorenzo," she said.

"I mean, this is what keeps us going, isn't it?" he said. "Art, music, all of the finer things. We can be such animals at times, but we are also capable of such beauty. We need this to keep us from becoming savages. This is what makes us reach for the stars, don't you think?"

"Yes," she said. It was true. It was hard to believe that all this could disappear. She looked around the room. All these masterpieces could be gone in the blink of an eye, turned to dust and rubble. It was too horrible to think of.

"Lorenzo, I can't dwell on that," she said. "I have a job to do, and I want to do it. Can you drive me somewhere in Montgomery County?"

He bowed again. "At your service, ma'am!"

"You can stop calling me, ma'am," she said. "I told you before, my name is Mercy. Just call me that."

"Say no more," he said. "Mercy it is."

They took a different route out of the museum, going through the main doorway and out onto the great plaza that overlooked the Benjamin Franklin Parkway. "Will you just look at that?" Lorenzo said, pointing out the view, which included the fountain at the foot of the steps, mirrored by another fountain ten blocks away, with the massive bronze statue of George Washington astride his horse, and the wide, straight parkway flanked by large trees awash in Fall colors, culminating in the rococo splendor of City Hall a mile away.

"Do you know this is modeled on the Champs-Elysees in Paris?" he said. "I've never been to Paris, but I can't imagine the view on the Champs-Elysees could be any better than this. Just look at it, Mercy! Why, the sky is so blue it looks like it goes on forever, and those trees, the bright oranges and reds and yellows, the way they give a golden glow to everything. It's a moment to remember, isn't it?"

"It is," Mercy said, taking it all in. "Especially when you describe it that way. You have the soul of a poet, Lorenzo, and the eye of an artist."

He shrugged. "I just have an appreciation for beauty. I don't like to let these moments pass without appreciating them."

Mercy looked at him as they went down the steps to the cab. He was a special man, she thought. She had never met a cab driver who expressed such thoughts. He was unique.

In the cab she gave him the address and he took off, winding his way along the East River Drive, with the Schuykill River on the left and the Victorian era statues and monuments of the Laurel Hill cemetery looming on the cliffs to their right. He had the radio tuned to the news station, and there was a tense report saying that our Ambassador to the United Nations Adlai Stevenson was going to meet with the U.N. Security Council that afternoon to address the missile crisis. Mercy felt her stomach tightening and her head throbbing with the tension that seemed to be emanating from the radio.

Lorenzo seemed to read her mind, and he switched the station to classical music. "I hope you don't mind," he said. "I would rather not listen to that."

"I don't mind at all," Mercy said.

They passed scullers on the river, oarsmen who were working their way down the river in the brilliant Fall sunshine. It was a peaceful scene, and it reminded Mercy of the famous Thomas Eakins painting of scullers on this very river, done almost 100 years ago. I wonder if there will be a day like this 100 years from now, she thought, when people will be rowing on the river?

Lorenzo was trying his best to dispel the mood of gloom that seemed to be lurking at the edges of this day. He rolled down the window and gave a running commentary about the sights of the city. He also regaled her with stories of his childhood, sang opera arias, told her the meaning of local slang, cracked jokes.

"How did you learn all this?" Mercy said. "You're a walking encyclopedia of Philadelphia history, art, music -- you're better educated than most of the art collectors I've met in California."

"Well, I didn't go to school for it," Lorenzo said, chuckling. "We didn't have money for a college education in my house. My Dad told me I could get a better education if stayed curious, kept my eyes and ears open, and I've always done that. I really like to read, listen to music, look at paintings and sculpture. I don't meet many people who like the things I do. Most people I meet in this cab just seem to want to live their lives focused on what's right in front of them. They don't see all the beauty around them, you know? They're afraid to look up, that's what my Dad said. He was always telling me to open my eyes. 'There are miracles right in front of your eyes, Lorenzo'. That's what he'd say."

"Your father sounds like an interesting man," Mercy said.

"Oh, he was," Lorenzo said. "I admired him so much, coming over here from the old country the way he and my mother did. Why, imagine that -- pulling up stakes from a place where your family's lived for generations, the only life you've ever known, and coming all the way across the ocean to this country, where it's all new, nothing like you've ever seen before. Do you know, he told me when he came here he didn't know what indoor plumbing was? He'd never seen a lightbulb, a telephone, certainly no moving pictures like Pops Lubin made. My Dad was from the mountains in Calabria, and they were living like people had done in the Middle Ages there. Still, he took a risk, coming here. It could have all gone sour for him."

"People did take a risk coming here," Mercy said. "But some of them were running away, you know. They had no choice." She thought of her father. Her mother had written a letter to her just five years before and told her the story of her father's past, how he'd killed a man in Ireland and came to America to run away from it.

"Doesn't matter," Lorenzo said. "Whether they were running away or not, they were all looking for something better. But they had to give up everything they knew, and there was no guarantee they'd find a better life here. Some of them didn't, you know. I knew old Italian people in my neighborhood who never learned English, never really felt at home here, missed the old country so much they were like shadow people, barely here at all. I used to feel sorry for them, poor souls. My Dad wasn't like that; he threw himself into the life here, and he enjoyed it. He was like a kid, always discovering new things to be excited about."

He put his arm out the window, and seemed happy, content to drive along in the glory of the October day. The trees across the river were a riot of colors -- gold, carmine, maroon, lemon yellow, and infinite shades of brown. It was a glorious day, and as they made their way out of the city and into the suburban farm country, the rolling hills and fields of corn, pumpkins, and squash added more color to the scene.

"It is imperative to enjoy every minute," Lorenzo said. "That's another thing my Dad told me, and I try to follow his advice. How about your father?" he said. "What was he like, if I'm not getting too personal?"

"He was a terrible man," Mercy snapped. She was surprised at the force of her reply, and there was a moment of embarrassed silence. "Oh, I guess he wasn't all bad. I have some good memories of him. A precious few."

Lorenzo cleared his throat. "I'm sorry. I just thought that, since you said he was an actor, maybe he was a man with a lot of personality. Fun-loving, you know? My Dad said some of the actors he knew at Pops Lubin's place were like that. We don't have to talk about him if you don't want."

"No, no," Mercy said. "I can talk about him. Doesn't bother me at all. I had some bad memories, but I'm over them. He was a fun-loving man, definitely. I remember him taking me to see the Christmas decorations in the shop windows on Market Street. He took me ice skating on the river when it froze one year, and we went for carriage rides, and he took me to the zoological gardens. He sang, too, beautifully, and he'd sing me to sleep some nights. He called me his precious little girl."

149

"There you go," Lorenzo said, smiling. "I can see you have some happy memories. Did he ever take you to the studio out here, Betzwood?"

It was like a black cloud had overshadowed them. All of a sudden Mercy felt queasy, and she could not talk. Lorenzo seemed to realize her mood had changed.

"I'm sorry," he said. "We don't need to talk about that. You know, there's an interesting historical fact that--"

"No," she said. "I can talk about it. My mother took my brother and me to the studio once, when I was about ten. It was a surprise visit. He wasn't expecting us at all. We saw some things. . . well, he betrayed us, that's all."

"I'm sorry," Lorenzo said. He was looking in the rear view mirror at her, and his eyes looked sad. "That's a terrible thing to happen to a little girl, discovering that her beloved father has feet of clay. Well, I guess you just have to move on, right? Forgiveness, that's what we all need."

"I've never been able to forgive him," Mercy said. "Not for ruining my childhood like that."

Lorenzo was pensive, his eyes wandering from the rear view mirror to the foliage outside. Finally, he said, "It's not too late, you know. Why, I talk to my Mom and Dad all the time, and they've been gone for years. I still talk to them, though, like they were sitting across from me at the breakfast table. I think you could just have a chat with your father and tell him you forgive him. We're all just human, you know, we do bad things all the time. Your name is Mercy, right? You should be able to give him mercy. Why, he could be suffering in Purgatory right now, in need of mercy."

"He can go to Hell," Mercy snapped. "I'm done with him, the lying bastard. I've washed my hands of him long ago."

Lorenzo fell silent again, and the only sound was the cab's engine and the rhythmic slapping of the tires on the asphalt road.

"I don't think our family ever really leaves us," he said, finally. "I guess I'm like the Chinese in how I think about that. I think the family, the ancestors, are all around us. I think you should make peace with him some day."

"That will never happen," Mercy said. "Now, I'm finished talking about this. I need some time to think."

"Certainly," Lorenzo said. He tuned the radio to the classical music station again, and turned up the volume, so the air was filled with the sounds of a violin concerto.

Lorenzo drove on in silence for the rest of the way. Once or twice Mercy caught him looking at her in the rear view mirror, but mostly he left her alone with her thoughts.

And she was thinking of her father. What would she find at the end of this journey? An image of him in an old silent film? The sound of his voice? Would that make everything all right? If she was honest with herself, she had to admit that there was a big hole in her heart where he had been. He had been her knight in shining armor and when she saw that he wasn't, that he was just a man with a hole in his own heart that he could not fill, she never got over it. All of her life had been a retreat, a going cold, a losing faith. She had never believed in anyone, not completely, for the rest of her life. Even at her first wedding, standing in front of a Justice of the Peace in Cincinnati, she'd had a part of her heart that wasn't truly participating. She'd known it, known that she wasn't giving herself completely to the man she was marrying, but that was because she couldn't.

And now here she was, driving along a road outside of Philadelphia on a jewel clear day in October, a day that could be her last day on Earth, a day when many people would want to be with their loved ones rather than anywhere else on the planet, and she, what was she doing? She had no loved ones to be with, she had only shattered dreams and broken hearts. She was doing a favor for her friend Nelson, but it was more than that, really. It was a prospect that filled her with dread and excitement at the same time: the possibility of seeing her father on film. What could she hope to learn from this? The man died more than 25 years ago, and she hadn't seen him for decades before that. He should have been gone, vanished from her life.

Except he wasn't. He was still there, his laughing face and his crooning voice, his warm embrace and his vitality, his humor and his physical grace. He was there every minute of every day inside her, and she could never get him out. He was there when she woke up in the morning and when she lay awake in the middle of the night, unable to sleep. He was part of her soul, and he had always been.

Lorenzo cleared his throat. "Excuse me, Mercy, but I think we're here. The number on this mailbox says 227, the same as what you wrote on your note."

CHAPTER TWENTY ONE

August 1970

Rosie was going home. It had been eight years and she had finally had her fill. It had been a wild, crazy ride and it felt like she had seen and done enough for three lifetimes. She'd made a lot of money, too, and sent a lot of it home to Pete.

But it was time. The longing in her heart was too much, the ache was bottomless. For a time she'd thought that James' love would heal her, but no, it was not enough. He had told her he was going to leave Elizabeth, move to America with her, but she didn't think he could do it. She looked into his eyes and saw he didn't have it in him.

Harry Helms told her he'd get her a job in New York or LA, but she didn't want that. She wanted Philadelphia, wanted to be back with her family. Pete was 24, and he was still getting into trouble, fighting with cops, getting fired from jobs. Her mother's letters were alarming. Plus, her mother was alone now. When her father died two years ago Rosie had promised her mother that she would move back within the year. She was past her deadline, and she knew she needed to get home.

The clincher was when she heard that Russo had died in prison. Her mother sent her the newspaper clipping. He had crossed the wrong people in prison, and he'd paid for it by being stabbed in his sleep one night.

So, there was nothing holding her back. She told James one night at dinner, and when he tried to tell her he was going with her, she put her finger on his lips and said, "No. Don't make promises you can't keep. You belong here, where your family has lived for generations. They need you. I'm from a different world, James, and I need to go back there. You stay here. Some day maybe I'll send Pete over to meet you. Until then, I'll go my way and you go yours."

He tried to protest but she had her mind made up. She had her plane ticket in her purse, and she was leaving the next day.

There was one detour, though. She was going to visit her grandmother's birthplace, Skibbereen.

It was amazing to think of it, that she had never been to Skibbereen in the ten years she lived in England. She had flown across the Irish Sea twice, to see bands in Dublin, but she'd never wandered south to County Cork. The time had been so crowded, so much had happened in the ten years in the UK, that she simply hadn't the time, strange as that sounded.

But now she felt the pull of it. She had been dreaming of it, had heard strange voices at odd times, at the edge of her consciousness, speaking a strange language. Was it Gaelic? Her grandmother had taken to reciting snatches of Gaelic in her old age, and the guttural sound of it stuck in Rosie's mind. Rosie had sat and listened to her stories when she was living in the Little Sisters of the Poor home, as the old woman seemed to go back so many years to her childhood. She spoke of cutting turf and laying it in stacks to dry in the sun; of walking miles over the hills and glens to the old stone church for Mass on Sunday; of the shanachies, or wandering storytellers, who would come and tell a scary story by the fire in exchange for a cup of tea and a hot meal. She muttered prayers in Gaelic, fingering her black rosary beads with her bent arthritic fingers, and occasionally she'd sing a mournful Gaelic song, her nasal tone like the sound of a sad violin.

"You'll go back, someday," she'd said. "Though, there's nothing left of the old world, I know. It's all gone, forgotten. But someday you must go back, if only to say a prayer by the old house I was born in, if, God willing, it is still there. Promise me you'll do that, girl."

And Rosie had promised, though she'd put it out of her mind these many years over here. She'd always known deep inside, though, that she couldn't leave without visiting Skibbereen. Now was the time.

So, she'd said goodbye to James, tears in her eyes but iron in her soul, and she'd given him one last kiss. The next morning she got up and took a cab to Heathrow airport for her flight to Cork, and while she was waiting to check in, there was a tap on her shoulder and she turned to see James.

"I'm coming with you," he said. He was dressed in a tan raincoat, a blue button down shirt open at the neck to reveal a burgundy cravat, and a blue blazer. His shoes were polished to a high shine, of course. He looked like an earl talking to a hippie. Rosie was dressed in her bell bottom jeans with the flowers stitched up and down the sides, sandals, and a coat that was made of feathers and spangles.

"You're not getting on that plane," she said. "I don't want you to. You cannot, James. This is foolish. Go home to your wife."

He smiled. "I want to be with you, not Elizabeth. I cannot bear to see you go."

"We discussed this already, James. I am going home, without you. I am just taking a short trip to Skibbereen for a few days, to see my grandmother's home town, but then I'm going back to America. And you can't come with me."

"We'll go over that later," he said. "Right now I'm just a sightseer, the same as you on this plane. Do you know I've never been to Ireland? My grandfather was killed there, back in the 19th century. He was a soldier, stationed in Cork. I would like to see where he lived. You're not the only one with a family history there, Rosie."

So he came and they took the short flight over the Irish Sea to the airport in Shannon, then took a train to Skibbereen and checked in to a little hotel on the outskirts of the city. The Irish clerk at the desk raised a skeptical eyebrow when James wrote "Mr. and Mrs. James McCarthy," in the book, but it wasn't, as Rosie originally thought, that he didn't believe they were married. He couldn't reconcile James, a proper English gentleman, having the last name McCarthy.

"Ye have relations in the area, then?" he said. "There are McCarthys everywhere in Cork. Though, ye don't look like one of the clan to me."

"I believe we're from a different branch of the family," James said. "An uncle or cousin went to live in England many years ago. So far back, I don't know all the details. Lost in the mists of time, you know."

In the room later, he said, "Serves me right for picking a name off a shop window. I should have known that if there was a McCarthy's grocer's shop then it would be a common name around here."

Rosie made love to him that night, but it was a disquieting experience that left her nerves jangled and raw. Where once it had been like the sun breaking through a mist, an opening of new vistas, like climbing to the top of a mountain and suddenly seeing a green valley spread out far below, now it was a closing off, a narrowing, an act poisoned by the mixture of lust and anger that they both seemed to be feeling. When it was over she slept fitfully, her mind troubled with fevered dreams and sounds just out of hearing. It was unseasonably hot for July, and the air in the room was close and heavy. Sometime before dawn Rosie had her dream again, of the music playing at the bottom of the hillside, and she ran down frantically, knowing the music was going to disappear before she got to the bottom of the hill. This time there was a discordant note, a jangling alarming sound, and when she got to the bottom it was like a slap in the face, the silence and the emptiness. She woke up feeling bruised inside, and she wanted only to be alone, away from James.

She felt better after breakfast, and then when she told the matronly desk clerk that her grandmother had been Rose Sullivan from an area called Gorteenalomane, the woman's face broke into a smile and she said, "I know the woman who's living in that house. It was sold twenty years ago, you know, my father was a barrister and took care of the paperwork for them. The woman who sold it had been living in England for a long time and the old place had fallen into a terrible state, roof falling in and all sorts of creatures living in it. I suppose that's after it passed out of your family's hands. The woman who bought it is English, by way of Australia. She's a lovely old soul, came here to retire with her husband, who passed away five years ago. They fixed the place up grand. I'm sure she'd be happy to see you."

The desk clerk insisted on lending her car to Rosie and James, would not hear of them calling a cab, and wrote out the directions on a map for them. Rosie took charge of driving the car, a boxy little dun colored Renault, and it rattled along on the stony roads as if it were going to shake itself to pieces. They had to stop many times for sheep or cattle crossing the road, and a couple of times Rosie almost drove into a ditch trying to avoid a placid brown heifer that stood splay footed in front of her and would not move.

They finally turned into a dirt lane pockmarked with ruts and holes, and Rosie floored it as they drove up a steep incline to the top of a hill. She made another turn and there it was -- a whitewashed stone house with a red roof and flowers growing from pots by each window, and a little garden with native wildflowers in it, awash today with purple butterwort and golden samphire.

In front of the house there was a tiny, cherubic woman standing with pruning shears in her hand, with a ruddy face and white hair in a bun.

"Welcome!" she said, coming over to the car immediately. "Frances Driscoll called ahead and said you were a delightful couple who had a connection to this house. My name is Felicia Barrett, and I live here. Do come in."

She was charming and voluble, eager to have someone to talk to, it seemed. She served them scones, and talked nonstop while an orange tabby cat curled up on her lap. Rosie tried to make conversation, but she was overcome by a sudden intense storm of emotions in this place where her grandmother had been born. She felt shaken to her roots. There was something powerful here, something primal. She struggled to come to terms with it, but it was unmooring her.

Felicia seemed to notice. "Are you all right, dear?" she asked. "You seem disturbed about something."

"She was close to her grandmother," James offered helpfully, patting her on the wrist. "It's a bit overwhelming, I suppose, to be in the house where your ancestor was born."

"Yes, indeed," Felicia said. "I understand completely. You must let me show you the rest of the house."

She took them through the place, babbling on about all the restoration work she and her husband had done, telling them in great detail about the sorry state of the place when they bought it, how there were birds' nests and even rats in the place, and a tree sprouting in the dirt floor of the kitchen. She wanted to take them upstairs to the second floor, which she and her husband had built, but Rosie stopped in her tracks when she saw the large room at the back of the house, with the stone hearth and the turf burning in the fireplace.

"What's this?" she said.

"Oh, this was the second most important room in the house, you know," Felicia said. "After the kitchen, the farm families spent most of their time here. It has a large fireplace, as you can see, and there were wooden beds up against the wall over there. This is where the family slept."

Rosie drew in her breath. She could feel the presence of the family here, could feel her grandmother as a little girl lying in a bed in that corner, listening to the songs and poems and stories her haunted mother told.

"She knew all the old stories," her grandmother had said. "Ach, the woman's head was full of that, all the poetry of the old times. You could listen to her, and the light of the fire would be glowing in her eyes, and she would make you feel you were living in the time of giants, fairy kings, and princesses. Sure, and it was magic to hear her talk. It was like she could see right into that other world."

Rosie was trembling, and her head was swimming. She tried to take a step forward but instead she sank to the floor. James caught her, and guided her to an overstuffed chair, where he sat her down gently.

"Good Heavens, is she all right?" Felicia said. "The poor thing, she looks very pale. I'll get her a glass of water." She scurried off to the kitchen, and when she was gone, James stroked Rosie's hair and whispered that everything would be all right.

But Rosie wasn't listening to his voice. She heard other voices, lots of them, all talking at once. They were talking in Gaelic, and she could not understand the words, but somehow she understood the intonations. There were children pleading with their mother for a treat, an old man saying his prayers with the weariness of a full day in the fields in his voice, a woman scolding her wayward son, a group of other women gossiping, a priest saying a prayer at a deathbed while a mourner wailed in the background, and so much more. The voices were all here, all the people who had lived here were still present, still here, insisting on their identity, their right to existence, clamoring for attention, trying to tell her something.

"What is it, Rosie?" James said. "What's the matter?"

"They're all here," she whispered, hoarsely. "All of them."

"Who?" he said. "Who is here?"

"The family. The people who lived here. All. Here."

160

"Here's some water," Felicia said, coming back in the room with a full glass. "Perhaps you're dehydrated, dear."

Her tinny voice seemed to drown out all the other voices, and they faded into the background as Felicia prattled on.

"I understand completely how this can happen," she said. "A young girl like yourself, I know you slim young things don't eat enough to keep a bird healthy. Watching your figure and all that. And then, there's the problem of drugs. You see, I live out here in the hinterlands of Cork, but I do keep up with what's happening in the world. I know there are people who smoke all sorts of strange substances, and they have visions and so forth. I worry about you young people, the lives you're leading."

"Oh, she's not on drugs," James said. "Nothing like that. I think she just had some sort of a spell."

"They were here," Rosie said, holding her head in her hands. She was losing the sound of their voices, and it was such a sad feeling. She wanted to hear them again.

"Who?" Felicia said. "Who was here?"

"The old ones," Rosie said. "I heard the voices of the people who lived here. My grandmother's family."

"Oh, them," Felicia said. "Yes, of course they're here."

"Have you heard them?" Rosie said.

"Why, yes dear," Felicia said. "I hear them quite a lot. Usually at night, when I'm in bed. I hear them down here squabbling about things. Or singing. Or telling stories in their language. It's actually quite nice, I think. Keeps one from feeling lonely."

"They're trying to tell me something," Rosie said.

Felicia chuckled. "Perhaps they are, although you'll have to figure that out yourself, won't you? I suppose they have some sort of message for all of us, if we could just understand it. And each one gets something different.

She clapped her hands. "You know what would be nice right now?" she said. "A cup of tea. That would do the trick." She went out in the kitchen and put a kettle on for tea, then came back in a few minutes with a tray and some cups and saucers, and poured tea for Rosie and James.

She sat across from them and sipped her tea and talked of the spirits as if it were the most natural thing in the world.

"I think this country is the most marvelous place," she said. "I felt it the first time I came to Ireland. Why, you can see traces of spirits in every glen, down every lane and mountainside, in the eaves of every house and sitting on the gateposts. You can hear strange music at dusk, and you see the most beautiful tableaus in the mists that cover the mountains. I think you are closer to the spirits here than anywhere else in the world."

James gave a wry smile. "Well, it must be a good thing for you," he said, chuckling. "I can see you'd never get lonely in a country like this. In fact, I wonder how you sleep at night with all the racket from the spirits."

"Oh, it's like a lullaby," Felicia said. "They lull me to sleep."

"I've never felt them like this," Rosie said.

Felicia stirred some sugar into her cup. "It's the country, I'm telling you. I think the veil between our world and theirs is very thin here. One can see right through it, at times. Oh, it does seem a magical thing, when one hears the sweet music and the sounds of their laughter. My husband swore he saw them clear as day once, dancing in a fairy ring at the bottom of a pasture, with a piper playing the most fetching music and the little people dancing so solemnly in their costumes of red and gold.

"It's what keeps me here," she said. "I miss my Henry terribly, but somehow I feel closer to him here. I think he's just around the bend in the road, waiting for me.

"I wish I knew what they were saying," Rosie said. "I've heard those voices before, but never so clearly."

James seemed bemused by the whole conversation. "I don't really believe in this nonsense, but if I did, I wouldn't think it would be all sweetness and light, you know. This land has seen a lot of bloodshed for centuries now. If there are spirits in this countryside, they're the spirits of people who've been killed in anger."

Rosie looked at him like he was an alien. He did not seem familiar to her anymore, and suddenly it was strange to think of him as the father of her son.

And then, clear as a bell, she heard: "Go."

Just one word, but it was so clear she looked around to see who'd said it. Felicia and James stared at her with blank faces, and she knew they hadn't heard it.

Rosie stood up. "I thank you," she said. "I could stay here for days talking to you. This is a subject that fascinates me. And besides, I feel my grandmother and her family here so strongly. But I must go. I realize now I must go."

She thanked the English woman for her hospitality, then took her leave. Outside in the car, she told James he could stay on in the hotel in Skibbereen, but she was leaving that night to go back to the Shannon airport, where her plane was leaving for America the next day.

"Darling, I'm coming with you," he said.

She kissed him on the lips, passionately, and said, "No. You belong here. We had a great fling, James, and we produced a fine boy. But it's all gone now. You can come over to Philadelphia some time later and meet him, or I'll send him over to meet you. But you and I are done. Have a great life."

CHAPTER TWENTY TWO

October 23, 1962

Lorenzo had pulled the cab into a long dirt driveway marked with a battered metal mailbox tilted at a crazy angle and the number "227" in red letters on it.

There were fields of corn in the distance, and closer there was a field dotted with orange, yellow, and green pumpkins and gourds, with a lattice of vines like a giant spider's net on the ground. At the end of the driveway was a dilapidated white and tan house, looking like it had been built in stages over a long time, and an even more dilapidated red barn behind it, with paint peeling from it and holes in its wooden sides. It had a large sign nailed to it that said "Antiques, Bought And Sold" in gold letters on a green background, but the paint was peeling and it was tilted at an angle. There was an ancient, rusted blue truck parked next to it, but it didn't look like it had been driven in years. The driveway was full of potholes, and the cab bounced as Lorenzo drove along it.

They pulled up in front of the house, and Lorenzo turned the car off. There was the sound of a radio coming from somewhere inside the house. There were rickety white rocking chairs on the porch, and a brown cat was sitting on one, regarding them with detachment.

"I guess this is the place," Lorenzo said.

"Yes," Mercy said. "I'm going to see if anyone is home. Wait here, please."

She got out of the car and went up the three creaky steps to the porch. The cat followed her with its eyes but did not move otherwise.

She knocked on the screen door three times. The inside door was open, and she could see a woman sitting in front of a large old-fashioned radio.

In a moment, the woman got up out of her chair and came to the door. She was small and round and walked with a cane. Her face, when it appeared behind the screen, was wrinkled, but she was wearing heavy makeup and she had red lipstick thickly applied. Her hair was jet black, and Mercy thought it was probably a wig.

"Yes," she said. "What do you want?" She enunciated her words very clearly, like an actress.

"I'm looking for Jonah Martin," Mercy said.

"Whatever for?" The woman's blue eyes narrowed and she looked at Mercy warily.

Mercy cleared her throat. "Henry Mortenson, from the Museum Of Art, sent me," she said. "I represent a collector in California, and he's interested in purchasing some prints of old films. He said you may have some I could look at. Is Jonah Martin available?"

The woman snorted. "Not anymore. No, he's not available anymore."

"I see," Mercy said. "When will he be back?"

This time she laughed harder, a barking, raucous chortle. "Oh, he's not coming back," she said. "Not unless he decides to come back and haunt me. He's dead."

"Dead?" Mercy said. "But Mr. Mortenson told me--"

"Oh, he wouldn't know," the woman said. "It just happened a week ago. Jonah just keeled over dead from a heart attack. Right in the middle of a pile of his beloved junk. I had him buried yesterday. Haven't had time to notify the newspapers or anything. I expect that Mortenson man will be snooping around here when he finds out. He and Jonah were two peas in a pod. More interested in collecting flea-bitten remnants of the past than anything else."

"I'm sorry for your loss," Mercy said.

"Don't be," she said. "He had his good qualities, but Jonah was a frustrating man. He lived in the past. He used to say he was born too late, and I think he was right. The man would have been happier if he was born 100 years earlier. He took a lot of time away from me with his obsession with history."

"Are you his wife?" Mercy said.

"My name is Esmeralda Atchinson Finney," she said. "I'm known as Esme. I wasn't born around here. I'm from Boston, and my mother's family came over two ships after the Mayflower. I was raised to be a proper lady." She looked toward the dilapidated barn and said, "My mother told me not to marry Jonah Martin, and sometimes I think I should have listened to her."

Her voice quavered, and she seemed to be on the verge of crying, but she snapped out of it.

"Now, if you don't mind, I'm going back to the radio," she said. "Goodbye."

Mercy was still hopeful, though. "Could I come in?" she said, boldly. "I don't mean to be forward, but I came all the way from California, and my client--"

"Have you listened to the news?" Esme said. "I can't believe you'd be interested in old films at a time like this."

"I know it's a difficult time," Mercy said. "But my client is really interested in those films."

Esme looked at her like she was a creature from the forest, a raccoon, say, who'd just showed up on her doorstep, stood up on its hind legs, and started talking.

"May I come in?" Mercy said, once again.

"No," Esme said, turning away.

"What's the harm in talking about something beautiful?" Lorenzo said, from the driveway.

The old woman turned and peered through the screen at him. "Who said that?"

"It was me, ma'am," Lorenzo said, taking his hat off and bowing. "I was just making the observation that maybe it's a better use of our time to talk about beautiful things rather than the ugliness on the radio."

She hesitated, then said, "All right." She opened the screen door and came out, shooed the cat off the rocker, and sat down. She looked at her watch. "You have five minutes. Start talking."

168

Mercy sat down on one of the other rocking chairs. She could see Lorenzo leaning against the side of the cab. "As I said, I'm interested in some films," she began. "I represent a collector who'd like to purchase some films from Siegmund Lubin's studio. I understand it was located near here."

Esme's face softened. "Betzwood? It was over there, about half a mile away," she said, pointing. "Jonah loved that place. It was abandoned for years. Now they're turning it into a community college. I heard about Betzwood my whole marriage. Jonah grew up on this farm, and he used to wander around that place as a kid, he and his friends. When he was a boy it was a working film studio, you know. They made hundreds of films there. He said it was magical." The cat had crawled up on her lap, and she was stroking the fur on its back meditatively.

"It must have been a great place for a boy to explore," Mercy said.

"Oh, yes. Jonah said he used to sneak over there and watch them work. It was wonderful to see all the actors and actresses in their costumes, with their makeup on, to watch the scenes they were shooting. They had whole battles over there, cowboys and Indians shooting at each other, oh, he said it was marvelous. Then it was over. Gone. Things crashed pretty quickly for Lubin when the War came. He had a lot of legal troubles, too, people like Edison suing him for stealing their technology, you know. They auctioned off some of the items from the studio, but there was still a lot of stuff lying around. Jonah used to bring home all sorts of things -- props, costumes, tools. He had the soul of a pack rat, that man. Never threw anything away."

"It's a good quality to have if you're in the antiques business," Mercy said.

"Antique business?" Esme said, laughing. "More like the junk business. Things that normal people throw away, he kept. Sometimes he made a few dollars on it, but lots of times he held on to it. He was addicted to the past, you see."

"The past is like a country that we travel through," Lorenzo said. "Some people don't want to look around, they just want to pass through it. Others want to settle down in it."

"You talk like a poet," Esme said.

"I'm just a man who pays attention," Lorenzo said. "To words, as well as to everything else around me."

"Well, you probably would have liked my husband," Esme said. "He paid attention, although mostly to the past. He distrusted newness, that man. Didn't like it at all. He was stuck in yesterday, I always said. I'll give you an example. I wanted to move to Florida, get away from these Philadelphia winters. He promised for years he'd do it, sell the business, but in the end he couldn't bring himself to part with all the junk. He used to say that everything in his collection had something to tell, and he knew all the stories."

"He sounds like a remarkable man," Lorenzo said. "Very sensitive to the life of objects, I can see."

"Ha!" Esme snorted. "Junk, all of it, and it was more important to him than moving to Florida. And now it's too late," she said, lifting the cat off her lap and getting up from the chair, then putting the feline down. "He's dead and gone, we never got to Florida, and now I'm stuck with all this junk. And the Russians are going to bomb us into oblivion. I think there's no point in continuing this discussion. Goodbye." She started to walk to the door.

"Wait," Mercy said. "Please. I've come all the way from California. Can't you just humor me for a few minutes? Whatever happens with the Russians is going to happen anyway. Talking to me isn't going to make a difference one way or the other."

"What do you want from me?" Esme said, her hand on the screen door. "I told you it's just junk."

"Yes, I heard that," Mercy said. "But about the films. Are there any films in your husband's collection?"

"Films?" Esme said. "I don't know. I guess there are some in the middle of all that trash. Jonah was interested in old films, I know that. He did have some of it stored in one part of the barn. I have no idea if it's what you're looking for."

"Can I see the films? Do you have them still?"

"What's your name?" Esme said. "You never told me your name."

"I'm sorry. It's Mercy Francis. I work for a man named Nelson Parnell."

She raised her eyebrows. "Nelson Parnell? The silent film star?"

"That's right," Mercy said. "Most people don't recognize that name these days."

"I'm sure they don't," Esme said. "That's because most people don't give a damn about the silent era, but that was where the true artistry was. I agreed with Jonah about that, if nothing else."

"I agree also," Lorenzo said, from his perch next to the car. "Those silent film stars had a presence, a majestic quality, that you don't see today. Gloria Swanson, Mary Pickford, Francis X. Bushman, Ramon Navarro, Douglas Fairbanks. They were larger than life, weren't they?"

Esme chuckled. "A cab driver who knows silent films. Will wonders never cease?"

"Oh, I love the old films," Lorenzo said. "I'm a big fan of them. My Dad introduced me to them. He was an immigrant, didn't speak the language very well when he first came over. That's why he enjoyed the silents, because he could figure out the story from just watching the actors."

"Jonah always claimed the old days of Hollywood were better," Esme said. "He wouldn't take me to the movies, because he hated the new stars. Oh, he didn't like rock n' roll, cars with fins on them, television. He wouldn't own a television. 'Radio's good enough for me,' he'd say. 'Ever listen to a radio drama? It leaves room for your imagination. You have to fill in the details yourself, from what the actors are saying.'"

"That's true," Lorenzo said. "Television takes some of the drama out of things."

"My husband used to say that all the time," Esme said. "You and Jonah would have gotten along just fine."

She appeared to be wavering, and Mercy pressed on. It had become very important to her to see those films. "Can we see the Lubin material? Would that be possible?"

Esme turned on her angrily. "Oh, what's the use? If these stupid politicians don't come to their senses, it could all disappear. We could all disappear. Doesn't that make you come up short? My husband spent a lifetime collecting things, and now it could all go up in one blinding flash, just disappear as if it never existed. No, I don't think I'm going to show anything to you. I'm so disgusted with human beings right now I don't want to have anything to do with any of you. Any race that would use a weapon like an atomic bomb, with all the destruction it's capable of, doesn't deserve to look at my husband's collection. Now, goodbye. I'm going back inside."

She started to move to the door, and Mercy's heart sank.

"You know, the way I see it, if this is our last night on Earth, there's nothing I'd rather do than look at some beautiful examples of Man's creativity and spirit," Lorenzo said. "I think you have an audience here that appreciates your husband's treasures, Mrs. Martin, so why not let us have a look?"

Esme's eyes seemed to fill up, and her hand trembled on the door handle. It was late afternoon, and the almost horizontal rays of sunlight cast a golden orange glow on everything. Esme's face shone with light, and she seemed to soften for a moment.

"Oh, all right," she said. "I guess you have a point. Might as well go look at all of Jonah's junk one more time. Follow me."

CHAPTER TWENTY THREE

December, 1974

Pete couldn't believe his eyes. He was waiting for his friends to show up at the Club LeRoux down by Penn's Landing, right in the shadow of the Ben Franklin Bridge, and he was getting ready for a normal Saturday night, checking out the girls in their sparkly lame dresses, and in walked a group of superfly looking guys with big Afros, and with them were a group of fine looking ladies. As soon as they came up to the bar he noticed right away that one of them was Betty Taylor. She had filled out a little, and she had curves in all the right places, and the skintight silver dress she had on showed them all off. She still had that creamy tan skin and almond eyes, though, and she moved with a panther's grace in her six inch heels.

When she came to the bar he didn't think she remembered him, and she sat down with an older black guy in a striped blue and white suit, black shirt and white tie, with a broad-brimmed hat with a white sash. The guy ordered two Johnny Walker Reds, and then he scanned the dance floor to see what was happening tonight. Within minutes he was gone, out on the floor doing the Latin Hustle with a blonde in a tight black dress who seemed glued to his pelvis. The other members of his entourage were out there too, all except for Betty, who was staring at Pete.

"You remember me?" Pete said.

She put her drink down. "Sure. You sat on my porch and talked to me about Luther. That was a long time ago, wasn't it?"

"It sure was," he said. "How are things going for you?" he said. "You look like you got it together." She was truly a vision, so much different than the simple girl he sat on the porch swing with.

She smiled. "Don't be fooled. This is just my disco look. I'm still the same inside. I'm a legal secretary, and these are the folks from my office. I work for Cicero Long's firm. That's him out on the dance floor. You know, the guy who finally got the trade unions in this city integrated? The one who got those stuffed shirts in all the old law firms to hire black attorneys?"

"How could I not know about him?" Pete said. "He was on the news for ten years straight, always with a big cigar in his mouth, at the front of a picket line. I haven't seen him lately. Guess there's no more picket lines needed, so he's out of a job."

She shook her head. "You always were so dense, Pete. The job of people like Cicero Long is not going to be finished for a long time. Racism runs too deep in this country."

"And he's your leader?" Pete said. "Look at him out there, with that white girl. He's almost in her pants. He's married, isn't he? Got a couple of kids?"

"You don't understand," she said. "He's got a lot of pressure in his life, and this is how he blows off steam. I can look past stuff like that, when I think of all the good he's done. I'm going to Temple law school because of him. Ten years ago they wouldn't have had me inside the building, unless it was to work in the cafeteria, or clean the restrooms."

Pete shook his head. "It doesn't matter. When you're married, you shouldn't do that. What's right is right."

She exhaled her cigarette, and stubbed it out in an ashtray. "You got it all figured out, huh? Got everything in its little box. You sound like a cop."

"I'm taking the test next week," he said. "I'll be a good cop."

"I'm sure," she said. "But if you rough up any black people, you'll have me to answer to."

"Don't worry," Pete said. "I don't want to face you in court. I'll be good."

He thought she was going to leave the bar, but instead she said, "You want to dance?"

"Sure," he said.

Then she hesitated. "But what about your leg? Are you still hurt?"

"No," he said, grabbing her arm and guiding her to the dance floor. "All I have left of that is a scar."

They went out to the floor just as the throbbing bass line of "TSOP (The Sound Of Philadelphia)" started up, and Betty glided into his arms to do the Spanish Hustle. Pete had been coming to this club for a year now, just as the new disco sound was taking hold, and he had learned all the right moves. He clasped her right hand with his left hand and put his right hand on the small of her back, and they glided as one, melding their bodies and letting the music flow through them. It was magic, heavenly. Pete had danced with many women, but this was something special. Betty seemed to know where he was going next, seemed to be able to tell before he even knew himself. She was so lithe, her body was so expressive, and she brought out a joy, an electric intensity, he hadn't felt in ages. Maybe never.

And she had a magnetism, a charge, that he felt through his skin. His hands tingled where they touched her, and he found himself getting hot, his temperature rising, with every move they made. He couldn't get over the feeling, it was like a door opened within himself. He was smiling in joy; somehow, for the first time in years, everything in his life made sense.

When it was over, he blurted out: "That was beautiful."

She nodded her head, as if she knew something magical had happened. They walked back to the bar, and Pete noticed his friends had arrived. They were standing at one end of the bar, and they all seemed to have stopped in the act of raising beers to their lips to look at Pete and Betty.

At the other end of the bar were Cicero Long and his entourage. They were also looking at Pete and Betty. The disco scene had only been going on for a year, and even though a lot of the clubs had mixed crowds, it was still a new thing for a white guy to dance with a black girl.

Pete walked Betty up to Cicero, who smiled and said, "You dance pretty good, for a white boy."

"This beautiful lady made me look good," Pete said. "You have good taste in legal secretaries."

"I have excellent taste, that's true," Cicero said. "I am known as a man of taste. Care to join me for a drink, young man?"

Pete thought about it, but he knew his friends were watching. They would ask too many questions already after seeing him dancing with Betty, and he didn't want the additional questions that would come if he shared a drink with a rabble rouser like Cicero Long. Plus, he knew what they were thinking: It's time to move on, if Cicero Long has showed up. They wanted to go to one of the other places they frequented.

"No thanks," he said, declining the drink. "My friends are waiting. We're supposed to go to another club."

"I can see that," Cicero said. "Yes, I can see they seem ready to go. Best not to keep your friends waiting. Nice to meet you."

Pete turned to Betty. "I want to see you again."

"You know where to find me," Betty said. "I'm still living with my mother, where you visited before."

"Tomorrow," he said. "Sunday afternoon. I have a car. We'll take a drive, go to a park. Would you like that?"

She sighed. "I don't know why I'm saying this, but yes. Pick me up at 2:00 sharp."

"Okay," he said. "See you then." He leaned over and kissed her, right there with everyone watching. It was a deep, full kiss and it sent a jolt through his body. He could have kissed her for ten minutes like that, but he was scared of so much energy running through his body, and he broke it off. He was out of breath, shook up, and she seemed the same way.

"I'll see you tomorrow," he said, and left.

CHAPTER TWENTY FOUR

October 23, 1962

Esme shuffled down the steps and across the driveway toward the barn. Mercy and Lorenzo followed after her. There was a skinny black dog who came up and nuzzled her leg and she murmured something to it, then it went back to playing with a stick it had found. The sunlight was fading, and there was a glow of anticipation in the air, a sense that something was about to happen.

Mercy had a tingling in her stomach, a growing excitement. She had not realized how important it was to her to see her father on film. All those years she had tried to forget him, and yet it had never gone away, her need to see him.

Lorenzo was walking beside her, his arm touching her gently with his fingertips as if he were guiding her, and she felt grateful for his presence. He was a kind man with inner strength, she knew, and it comforted her to have him here.

When they got to the barn Esme opened a creaky wooden door, then reached inside and turned on a light. Inside it was complete chaos. There were piles everywhere: furniture, toys, bicycles, a couple of brass four poster bed frames, ottomans, chairs, racks of gowns and suits, books piled on top of books, paintings of every description and color, silverware in boxes, stacks of 78 RPM records, plates, cups, movie posters, porcelain dolls, musical instruments, all piled together in heaps.

"This is amazing," Lorenzo said. "What a treasure trove!"

Esme looked at him skeptically. "I guess you could call it that. As you can see, Jonah loved collecting things, but he wasn't so good at organizing them. His system was scattershot, at best."

It was like being in the world's largest playroom. There were narrow aisles winding through the barn, and huge shelves against the wall, crammed full of anything that had caught Jonah Martin's eye. The fading light from a skylight gave everything a soft, magical glow.

"Look at this," Lorenzo said, standing by a rack of costumes. "Cowboy clothes!" He held up a wide-brimmed white Stetson hat, a red bandana, and a holster with a gun. He quickly tied the bandana around his face, put on the hat, and pointed the gun at them. "Reach for the sky, ladies, this is a stickup!" He tried to look stern, but his eyes crinkled with laughter.

"You don't make a very believable outlaw," Mercy said, chuckling. "I wouldn't be afraid of you at all."

He took off the bandana. "Yes, I guess I'm not the cowboy type. But here, look, wouldn't you look so grand in this gown?" He held up a sky blue gown, covered in ruffles and lace, and ran over and held it in front of Mercy. "Look at that! Wouldn't you look elegant in this? Why, I can just imagine you dancing in some beautiful ballroom with an orchestra playing and waiters in tails serving tall glasses of champagne."

"Your friend has quite an imagination," Esme said.

"Yes," Mercy said, chuckling. "This place brings out that side of him."

180

"Oh, it's a place of dreams, isn't it?" Lorenzo said. "These were the raw materials that the studio used to create grand dreams. It was really a dream factory, wasn't it?"

"Yes," Esme said. "I guess you could call it that. Dreams. My husband spent his life chasing dreams of the past."

"Well, this is all nice," Mercy said, "but do you know where he kept the films?"

"Whatever he had would be upstairs," Esme said. "He had a second story, and he kept the more valuable stuff up there, locked away."

She led the way up a wooden staircase that creaked as they went up it. Upstairs things were a bit more organized. There were rooms with gray metal filing cabinets against the walls, boxes stacked neatly, and large black steamer trunks in rows. Esme led the way to the last room at the end of a hall, opening a door to get inside, then switching on a light.

"This is where he kept the films," she said. "I helped him to organize it a bit, catalogue what he had, you know. That was years ago. I haven't been in here in a while, so I'm not sure where everything is."

She scanned the room, trying to place everything. Finally, she pointed at a large steamer truck against the far wall. "Over there. I think the Lubin films are over there."

Mercy's heart leaped. She felt nervous, on edge. What would she see? She had no pictures of her father, so all she had to go on was the memory she'd been carrying around for years. Would it match up with the reality on the old film?"

181

Esme went to a hook on the wall that had a large key ring on it, then bent down and started trying the keys on the padlock on the trunk. There was a name stenciled on the side of the trunk in white letters: "Lubin". Esme tried one key after another, while Mercy's heart pounded, and she felt her knees shaking. Lorenzo seemed to notice that she was agitated, and he put his hand on her shoulder, which helped to calm her.

Finally, Esme found the right key. It turned in the lock, and the padlock opened. She pushed open the lid of the trunk, and immediately there was a chemical smell that wafted up.

Inside, there were old canisters of film, but they looked rusted. They had labels that said, "Betzwood Studios" stenciled on them in black letters. Esme picked up one of the canisters. It was metal, and she unscrewed the top of it. Inside, there was a sharp, acid smell, and there were flakes of film that looked gooey and had white spots on them.

"It's ruined," she said. "The nitrate in the film has broken down. It happens to old films. From the smell in this trunk, they're probably all ruined."

"Oh, no," Mercy said. "I was hoping--"

"I told that crazy old man," Esme said, shaking her head. "I told him over and over to keep these things in a temperature controlled vault. He never listened, the old fool. Too busy collecting more junk to take care of what he already had. I'm sorry."

Mercy felt like she'd been punched in the stomach. She realized how important this had been to her. She had believed she was going to see her father again, even if it was only a few seconds of him on a faded black and white film. It was devastating to realize it was not going to come true.

"Are these the only ones?" she said. "Don't you have any more?"

"These are the only films from Betzwood," Esme said. "Jonah never found very many of them. The studio was only here for a couple of years. It was a long time ago. Most of Lubin's films were destroyed in a fire at his Philadelphia studio. There aren't many prints that have survived. I'm sorry."

Mercy could barely speak. She felt the need to sit down, so she went and sat down on the nearest steamer trunk. She felt lost, bereft. Lorenzo came and put his hand on her shoulder once again.

"Are you all right?" he said.

"I thought I would see my father," she said. "I guess I was hoping to."

Lorenzo turned to Esme to explain. "Her Dad worked at the Betzwood studio. He had bit parts in a few films. She thought maybe she'd get a glimpse of him."

"I'm sorry," Esme said. "These old films are fragile. They don't store well. You see that it didn't even say the name of the film on the canister. Nobody thought about preservation when they made these things. They just threw them in a can and left them."

"Yes, I know," Mercy said. "I just thought something would have lasted, even if it was only a few seconds. It meant a lot to me."

"Nothing lasts forever," Esme said shaking her head. "That's what I used to tell Jonah. I don't understand why people get so fixated on the past. People try to preserve the past, mummify it, but it never lasts. It slips through our grasp. I thought he'd realize that. He was trying to keep his childhood alive, I guess. Damn fool man, wasting his life on this stuff." She passed her hand about the room, taking in all the filing cabinets, boxes, and trunks.

Mercy was still stunned. She felt like she'd fallen off a balcony, and it was going to take a while to get her bearings again.

"So that's it?" she said. "That's all you have?"

"That's the only place Jonah had films from Lubin," Esme said. "Like I said, there weren't very many of them around."

"Most of us don't make a place for these things in our lives," Lorenzo said. "So the past vanishes into the rear view mirror, and it's gone."

"Can't hold on to it, that's for sure," Esme said. She clapped her hands. "Well, let's improve the mood, shall we? I may not have any silent films to show you, but I can crank up the old gramophone and play some records from back in those times."

Mercy sat there stunned, immobile, while Esme rooted around in a corner, then came back with a wooden box with a crank on its side and a metal piece attached that looked like the bell of a trumpet. She set the gramophone on a steamer trunk, then turned the hand crank a few times vigorously. She went to a filing cabinet and opened a drawer, reached inside and took out an LP record from a cardboard sleeve.

"I have no idea who this is, or what the song is," she said, "because Jonah bought these records at an estate sale, and none of them have labels. Let's see what we have here." She placed the disc on the gramophone, gently guided the needle into the groove on its surface, and suddenly the room was filled with sound.

It was a piano playing a soulful, slow melody, and then a high, clear tenor voice began singing "Dear Old Skibbereen".

Oh father dear, I oft-times hear you speak of Erin's isle

Her lofty hills, her valleys green, her mountains rude and wild

They say she is a lovely land wherein a saint might dwell

So why did you abandon her, the reason to me tell?

Oh son, I loved my native land with energy and pride

Till a blight came o'er the praties; my sheep, my cattle died

My rent and taxes went unpaid, I could not them redeem

And that's the cruel reason why I left old Skibbereen.

That voice! It was like a knife to Mercy's heart. That clear, high tenor voice. It was her father's voice. Some long buried memory surfaced with the suddenness of a chill. She'd heard him sing that song so many years ago, as a child. It came back with terrible vividness. She was at Willow Grove Park, where her father had taken the family on the train for a Sunday outing, far out in the suburbs. It was summer, a beautiful June day with families promenading in their summer clothes, and James had taken his little family out in a rowboat on a lake that shimmered like glass. He had

185

taken his jacket off and was sitting in his shirtsleeves and his Panama hat, beaming his wide smile and talking about how grand the afternoon was, when he broke into song. His voice was so clear and pure that people in other boats on the lake stopped and listened, rapt smiles on their faces. It was obvious he gloried in their attention, basking in it like a dog stretched out in the sun.

And then it happened. He finished the song, the last note ringing in the air for a moment or two longer, and then a man in a nearby rowboat called, "Peter Morley is it? I'd recognize that tenor voice anywhere. Why haven't ye been back to the saloon to sing those beautiful ballads?"

Her father's face turned chalk white and he looked as if he wanted to dive into the water and disappear.

"Why, I think you're mistaken, my good fellow," he said, trying to recover his composure. "My name is not Peter Morley, and I'm not in the habit of singing in saloons."

The other man, who had rowed several yards closer by now, and had the rough and ready look of a teamster or a piano mover on his Sunday outing, with a young ruddy-faced Irish girl sitting across from him, said, "Faith, haven't I listened to that voice many a Saturday evening not ten years ago? I'm not mistaken one bit, Peter, me boy. I always wondered what happened to ye. The boys at the saloon are missing ye all these years. It'd be a blessing if ye'd come back. Old Paddy Brogan would be glad, I'm sure -- he always sold more whiskey when ye were singing!" He laughed heartily, showing a mouth with several missing teeth.

"James, what is he talking about?" Mercy's mother said. "Do you know this man?"

186

"Not at all, my dear," Mercy's father said. He tipped his hat to the man, and said, "I'm quite sorry, but I'm afraid you're mistaken. I've never sung in a saloon in my life. Good day."

He rowed furiously away, leaving the man gaping at them with his mouth open.

Mercy knew now, looking back on it, that her father had thought he was far enough away from Paddy Brogan's saloon that no one would recognize him. When the Irishman in the rowboat identified him, it had almost shattered his double life.

But now he was here.

He was here in the room now, his voice filling the air with its aching sweetness. She felt hot tears come to her eyes. It was so cruel, what he'd done to her all those years ago, so heartless and cruel. To deceive them all like that -- why?

Lorenzo sat next to her and put his hand on her knee. "Is that him?" he said. "Is that your father?"

"Yes," she said, struggling to keep from crying. "He must have made some recordings. He had a fine voice, and people always told him he should be on the stage. I guess he made a recording that we didn't know about. There was a lot we didn't know about him."

"That's your father?" Esme said. "Are you sure?"

Mercy shook her head. "I am sure. I haven't heard that voice for fifty years, but I am as sure as I'm looking at you right now. It's him."

"You don't seem happy to hear him," Esme said, puzzled.

"Oh, I'm happy and sad at the same time," Mercy said. "It's complicated."

"Listen to that sound," Lorenzo said. "It's like the singer is right here in the room."

"The gramophones were like that," Esme said. "There was something special about that old recording technology."

"Your father had a beautiful voice," Lorenzo said, moving his hands in time to the music. "Just listen to it. There's a lot of sadness in it, Mercy. A longing for his homeland, don't you think?"

He was right. There was an ache in that voice, a soul-longing that grabbed you and didn't let go. He sounded equal parts lost, angry, bereft, and mournful. It was like he was singing right to her, to Mercy. Somehow, as hurt as she felt, there was also a note of understanding. For the first time, she had a glimpse into his soul. She could see what a lost, damaged, hurting creature he was. She realized with a start that he had been younger than she was now when he made this recording, probably not even 50. He'd killed a man so many years before, and had been running from it all that time. He had lied to and betrayed everyone who was close to him, and he could not get away from his guilt and shame, all of it growing heavier with each new lie.

When the last note rang out, and there was nothing but the scratching of the needle on the record, Esme took the disc off, put it back in the blank cardboard sleeve, and gave it to Mercy. "Here," she said. "This belongs to you. I have no idea who Jonah got this from, but I feel you should have it."

"Thank you," Mercy said.

"I could root around and see if there are any other records here your father made," Esme said. "But it could take me hours, because Jonah never had much of a filing system. As you can see, it's pretty disorganized here."

"No," Mercy said. "Thank you, but I've heard enough. I think I'll go now."

She felt strangely calm, even serene. The gnawing in her was gone. She had heard his voice, and he'd come back to her for a few minutes, long enough to make her understand the pain and sadness and confusion and terror in his life. Long enough to make her hear the cry of his soul, coming out through his voice.

And suddenly her need was gone. She could let him rest in peace now.

She stood up. "Lorenzo, can you take me back to the hotel? I feel tired, and I'd like to go back."

"Your wish is my command," Lorenzo said.

"What about the films?" Esme said. "You said there was a collector who wanted to find some of the Lubin films."

"I'll call him tonight, and give him an update," Mercy said. "If he wants me to stick around and do some more digging, I will. It's up to him."

"Well, you can call me if you want to come back," Esme said, leading them down the steps to the first floor. "I mean, look at this mess," she said, pointing to the mass of objects piled everywhere. "I have to get rid of it somehow." She shook her head.

"He told me we were going to move to Florida, but instead I'm stuck here with this junk."

Outside, in the driveway, the sun had just gone down, and the sky in the west was still awash in red and orange, shading to deep blue directly above them, where the first stars were coming out.

"It's a beautiful night, isn't it?" Lorenzo said, looking up at the first stars.

"I bet it's even more beautiful in Florida," Esme said. "Oh, I guess it's nice even here. I wonder how many more of these nights we'll see."

"Very many, I hope," Lorenzo said. "I hope this is the start of a new era, a time of hope and peace for all mankind. Isn't that a great idea to contemplate?"

"I'd give everything I have in that barn for the guarantee of one more year," Esme said. "But I guess it doesn't work that way, does it? Well, it was nice meeting you two."

She shuffled off towards the house, and Lorenzo held the door of the cab open for Mercy.

Inside the car, Mercy was alone with her thoughts. She felt like she had come to the end of a long road, and she was exhausted from her journey. She was not paying attention to where Lorenzo was driving. Her head was crowded with memories, and she let them occupy her thoughts. It seemed she finally understood her father, after so many years. It was almost too much to grasp.

Lorenzo looked in the rear view mirror and said, "I hope you don't mind, but I was out here once years ago, and I found this place where you can look out over the city. I thought it was an appropriate night for that."

Mercy realized he had stopped the car, and they were parked at the top of a hill that dropped off steeply and overlooked the lights of the city.

"Where are we?" Mercy said.

"It's a place near Chestnut Hill," Lorenzo said. "It's the highest point in Philadelphia. I've been here before, and I enjoyed the view. I thought you'd like to see it."

"I don't know," Mercy said. "I think I'd just rather go back to the hotel."

"Just for a minute?" Lorenzo said. "It's a beautiful view. I think you'll enjoy it. Why not take a look?"

"I think you missed your calling, Lorenzo," Mercy said, laughing. "You would make a good salesman. You're very persuasive. Okay, I'll get out, but just for a minute."

Lorenzo got out and came around and opened the door for her. She stepped out of the car and they walked to a small wooden fence at the edge of the cliff. You could see for miles -- Mercy could make out the City Hall tower, the Art Museum alone on its bluff, the ribbon of the Schuykill River reflecting the lights from the city, cars motoring down Broad Street. It looked like a blanket of stars had been thrown over the city, with lights twinkling from all directions.

"You're right, it's beautiful," Mercy said, taking it all in. "What a shame if it all disappears."

"Yes, it's a terrible thought, but that's what gives it more beauty," Lorenzo said. "It could all pass away in the blink of an eye, like a snowflake that melts in your hand. But nothing last forever, you know. All those people down there, if they don't die from a Russian missile, that's a good thing, but they'll still go about their business the same as ever, running around from one thing to another, getting caught up in what's right in front of their noses, instead of looking around at all this beauty. People have it all wrong. The beauty of the moment, Mercy, that's what it's all about. This moment now, that's what we should appreciate. Everything else is meaningless, in spite of what people think. This moment is where God is."

Mercy shook her head. "Lorenzo, you constantly amaze me. You're as much of a philosopher as you are a cab driver."

Just then a shooting star arced across the heavens. Mercy felt a thrill, and she couldn't help but smile.

Lorenzo turned to her, and put his hand on hers. "I would like to kiss you, Mercy. Would you mind if I did that?"

"Not at all," she said. "Not at all."

Lorenzo embraced her and kissed her tenderly, his lips tasting sweet on hers. Mercy was surprised and thrilled by his tenderness, and yet there was a deep strength that she could feel emanating from him. He pulled her close, closer, closer, and it suddenly dawned her, as suddenly as a shooting star falling from the heavens, that she had finally found a man to love.

CHAPTER TWENTY FIVE

May 7, 1976

Rosie looked around the cemetery and took it all in: the freshly dug grave, the rich smell of the earth, the flowers blooming in the May sunshine. The small knot of mourners, mostly people from the neighborhood and some that knew Lucy from her years in the Civil Rights movement, left their cars and moved across the broken ground to the open gravesite.

Pete had his arm around her, and on the other side was his girlfriend Betty, tall and elegant in her long black coat.

"How are you doing, Mom?" Pete said. "Are you okay?"

"Sure," Rosie said, squeezing his arm. "I'm okay. As well as can be expected, I guess."

At least I'm here, she thought. I wasn't here when my Dad died. But she was home now, and she'd nursed Lucy through her final illness, singing to her every night, reading books to her, praying with her when the old woman seemed to need it. She'd taken time off from her job as a legal secretary in the last month and spent every minute with Lucy. It was something she was grateful for, that she'd had the chance to be with her mother like that.

The priest, a beefy man in a cassock and white surplice, sprinkled holy water on the casket, read some prayers, and said a few words about the eternal reward this good woman had already gone to. Rosie didn't cry; she had already been through that. She had a feeling that Lucy and Paul were looking down on her, so when the priest asked if anyone wanted to say anything, Rosie broke into

"Amazing Grace". It just seemed right, and she put her whole heart and soul into it, hitting the notes with fervor.

Amazing Grace, how sweet the sound,/ That saved a wretch like me./ I once was lost but now am found,/ Was blind, but now I see. . .

She gave herself over to it, throwing her whole soul into the words, singing at the upper register of her voice, not caring that her voice was on the edge of cracking when she hit the high notes.

And when she finished with. . .

Yea, when this flesh and heart shall fail,/ And mortal life shall cease,/ I shall possess within the veil,/ A life of joy and peace.

The final note rang out over the quiet hillside like a bell ringing, and seemed to echo in the ears of everyone there.

There was a moment of silence, and then everyone applauded, and someone said, "That was beautiful." The priest nodded his head and then the funeral director gave out white roses to everyone, and they filed by the casket one by one and dropped the rose on it.

It was over. A few people came up and hugged her, telling her what a good woman her mother was, and she nodded and thanked them for coming. Then it was time to go. She moved off with Pete and Betty, starting back to the car, when there was a tug on her arm.

She turned to see a familiar face.

"Rosie, people always told me you could sing, but I never heard you before. You are amazing, girl."

It was the Dittybopper. The familiar slicked back hair was gone, now his hair was in a modified shag, falling over his ears and clumping at the back of his neck, but somehow it still looked neatly combed and sprayed. He was wearing a teal blue suit with a white shirt open all the way to the top of his chest, where a silver cross was flashing in the sun. He was wearing his sunglasses, and he was chewing gum.

Rosie hugged him, and said, "What are you doing here?"

"I got a network like you wouldn't believe, darling," he said. "I hear things, lots of things. And I'm a loyal cat, remember? I don't forget my own. I heard your mother passed away, and I wanted to show my respect. Is this your boy?" he said, pointing to Pete.

"That's my son Pete," Rosie said. "And his friend Betty."

"Nice to meet you," the Dittybopper said, shaking their hands. "It's been a long time, but I remember your mother working at Russo's Diner. I used to go there every morning for the eggs and bacon. They had the best coffee in Philly."

"A lot has happened since then," Rosie said.

"Right," the Dittybopper said. "Time waits for no man, right? Listen, can I talk to you? I have something to say."

"Now?" Rosie said. "Here?"

"What better place?" the Dittybopper said. "I mean, I have a proposition to make and maybe this is the place for new beginnings, don't you think?"

"We just got finished a funeral," Pete said. "I don't think--"

"It's okay," Rosie said. "He's an old friend. I'll meet you back at the car."

Rosie watched Pete and Betty leave, then turned and said, "What do you want?"

The Dittybopper took off his glasses. His eyes, small and vulnerable, blinked in the sun. "Do you mind if we walk over to that tree?" he said, pointing to a tall oak tree that stood on a bluff. It was a majestic tree with a thick trunk and spreading branches, and it looked at least a hundred years old.

"Sure," Rosie said. She walked the fifty yards or so to the tree with him, then waited for him to speak.

"I come here sometimes," he said. "My mother is buried near here. Never knew my Daddyo. He lit out a long time ago. My mom believed in me, though. She convinced me I could do anything. I come here when I want to talk to her again. I could have used her in my life the last ten years."

"The British Invasion wasn't so good for you, was it?" Rosie said.

"Good?" he said. "It was like a nuclear bomb in my world. Overnight, the whole industry changed. I went from being a comer, a guy on his way up, to a square, an old fogey, a has-been in the time it took to listen to one Beatles song." He ran his hand through his hair. "Man, I never saw it coming. I thought I was the hippest cat around, the man who had the golden ears. I could listen to a song and tell you within the first ten seconds if it was going to be a hit. I met Sinatra, Dean Martin, all those guys. I had my own TV show for awhile, did you know that?"

"That must have been after I left for England," Rosie said.

"England!" he said. "I wish that country had never been invented. You know the first time I heard the Beatles, a friend of mine had a 45 of 'I Want To Hold Your Hand', and when he put it on the turntable I said, 'Those guys won't last a minute. American teens won't listen to that crap.' Boy, was I wrong."

"A lot of people were," Rosie said. "I called everybody I knew over here and told them about the Beatles, but nobody listened. I called you, remember? You didn't want to hear about them."

He put his hands up. "I know, guilty as charged. And I've paid for it. I had to get a job selling radio time just to pay the bills. Me, the Dittybopper, selling ads for dry cleaners and pizza shops on the radio! It's a real comedown."

"I'm sorry," Rosie said.

"It's okay. I'm coming back. The Dittybopper is making a comeback, girl! Have you heard of the Oldies format? It's something new in radio. All the classic songs from the 50s and 60s that I used to play. It started on the West Coast, after that movie 'American Graffiti' came out. Now, there's a wave, a groundswell, and people are ready to hear my music once more. I'm gonna climb that mountain again!"

He seemed so full of bravado, standing there puffing out his chest, that Rosie had to smile. "Good!" she said. "I'm happy for you. But is that what you wanted to tell me? That you're making a comeback?"

"Well, that's part of it," he said. "Look, I know this is a bad time to talk to you about work stuff, but I need someone I can trust to help me get back on my feet. I'd like to hire you."

Rosie was shocked. "Hire me? I haven't even seen you for years. How could you possibly want to hire me? You don't even know me."

"No, that's where you're wrong, pretty lady," he said. "I know you. I know you're a standup kind of person, somebody who's hip to right and wrong. You stood up to Gaeton Russo, when it was a stone dangerous thing to do. I know you were in the music biz in London, when it was the music capital of the world, and you can spot talent. I just found out you have a terrific voice, too. I think you can help me to get back on top, and I want to offer you a job."

"Doing what?" Rosie said.

He straightened his shoulders, and some of the old swagger came back as he jabbed the air with his finger and told her his plans.

"I got big ideas. I'm back to doing record hops, just like in the old days. It's starting small, but that's okay, it just gives me room to grow. I'm working Sunday nights at a bar in town, and I have Mondays and Wednesday nights at a fire house in New Jersey. More people are coming each week. They know they'll get the true oldies from me, because I still got my record collection, and it's solid gold, honey!" He was snapping his fingers, and his speech was getting that staccato rhythm back.

198

"Great," Rosie said. "I hope it works for you. But how do I fit into that?"

"I need an assistant. I need somebody I can trust, because the record business is a snake pit, you know that. I'm gonna build this business up, but I want to do it right this time. Once I start making my move, there'll be all sorts of slimy types trying to get a piece of me, just like before. I need somebody who can steer me through that, separate the good guys from the bad ones, and help me to make the right decisions. I need somebody who knows the industry, but who has a good head on her shoulders."

"And you think that's me?" Rosie said. "I've never been accused of having a lot of sense."

"No, you're perfect," the Dittybopper said. "I'm sure of it. Come on, Rosie, you know you want to get back in the business, don't you? The Dittybopper is coming back from exile, honey, and you can be part of it!"

"No, no, no," she said, shaking her head. "I have a good job. I'm a secretary at a law firm. I get paid good money, and I have health insurance, good benefits. My life is settled, for the first time in years. Why would I want to get back in the crazy record industry?"

He smiled. "Because music is in your blood. I heard you sing back there. You've got talent, and in another time you'd have been a star yourself. And I understand from my sources that you had a grandfather who sang Irish ballads, and had a local following. It's in your genes, darling."

"No," she said. "I don't think so. It's been nice talking to you, but--"

"Bobby Juliano's singing again."

"What?" Rosie said. "Bobby? The kid who--""Yes," the Dittybopper said. "The one that Russo sliced open like a sausage. He stopped singing for a long time, went back to hauling those crates of fish around at the market, but in the last year he got his boys together and they've been singing at weddings, bar mitzvahs, local stuff like that. He's still got the pipes, Rosie, and he has a following. I got big plans for him -- I'm gonna put together oldies revues, get some of the classic groups to come out and do some shows, and Bobby's going to be a part of that. Can you imagine? The casinos have their eye on Atlantic City, it won't be long before they'll be opening shop down there, and they're gonna need entertainment. I'll package these oldies revues and those guys in Atlantic City will be happy to sign them up. I'll be back on top, baby!"

Bobby Juliano. Rosie had always wondered what happened to him, if he had ever gone back to singing. She could still hear his soulful voice in her mind, the way it trembled with emotion during the slow songs. It was a tragedy what happened to him, and if the Dittybopper could help him. . . After all, he was born to be a singer; talent like that should be heard.

She sighed. "Bobby Juliano? You sure?"

"Absolutely. I just talked to him yesterday. He excited. He's ready, willing and able, he's going to put his cards on the table, he's ready to come back and bop at the Dittybopper's hops, he's --"

Rosie laughed. "Enough with the rhymes!"

"No problem," the Dittybopper said, holding his hands up. "I get excited and I can't help myself. But what do you say, Rosie? Will you do it?"

200

Rosie said the only thing she could say. "Yes."

THE END

THE END OF BOOK FOUR

This is the fourth of seven books in the Rose Of Skibbereen series. Look for the other books on Amazon at amazon.com/author/johnmcdonnell.

A word from John McDonnell:

I have been a writer all my life, but after many years of doing other types of writing I'm finally returning to my first love, which is fiction. I write in the horror, sci-fi, romance, humor and fantasy genres, and I have published 24 books on Amazon. I also write plays, and I have a YouTube channel where I post some of them. I live near Philadelphia, Pennsylvania with my wife and four children, and I am a happy man.

My books on Amazon: amazon.com/author/johnmcdonnell.

My YouTube channel:

https://www.youtube.com/user/McDonnellWrite/videos?view_as=subscriber

Look me up on Facebook at: https://www.facebook.com/JohnMcDonnellsWriting/.

Did you like this book? Did you enjoy the characters? Do you have any advice you'd like to give me? I love getting feedback on my books. Send me an email at mcdonnellwrite@gmail.com.

Find all the "Rose Of Skibbereen" books here:

amazon.com/author/johnmcdonnell.

Printed in Great Britain
by Amazon

25317995R00118